A Groom for Christmas

by

Cara Marsi

PUBLISHED BY:
The Painted Lady Press

A Groom for Christmas
Copyright @ 2013 by Carolyn Matkowsky
Print ISBN: 978-1493720422
Kindle ASIN: B00G03I5UI

ALL RIGHTS RESERVED. No part of this book may be used or reproduced in any manner, or by any means (electronic, mechanical, photocopying, recording, or otherwise) without the prior written permission of the copyright owner, except in the case of brief quotations in reviews or critical articles.

This book is a work of fiction and all characters exist solely in the author's imagination. Any resemblance to persons, living or dead, is purely coincidental. Any references to places, events or locales are used in a fictitious manner.

"A Groom for Christmas is a fantastic, feel-good read from a top-notch author!" ~ NY Times & USA Today Bestselling Author, Sandra Edwards

I loved this book......The situations and drama that follows is so real life you sometimes forget that these are make believe characters and not a true life story....The author did such a awesome job with drawing you into this story and keeping your attention page after page trying to see what would happen next....NetGalley Reviewer CarternAlexsmommy

....This one is a great, feel-good story with lots of Holiday spirit....Amazon Reviewer WestCoastBookLover

A Groom for Christmas is a delightful "Hallmark Christmas" love story. The chemistry between Jake and Graceann crackles like a Yule log....Amazon Reviewer J Morgan

What a perfect way to start getting in the mood for the holidays!....Amazon Reviewer Rebecca S. Burkhart

Jake and Graceann were a couple I cheered for from the first chapter....I'm a huge Cara Marsi fan and this book goes to the top of my list of favorites of hers! It's a fast read, with lovable characters that stole my heart....Amazon Reviewer Betty Boop Boop

"Great second chance at love story - with a really hot bad boy hero! I really loved this offering from Cara Marsi. It was fast paced and extremely well written. Strong, multifaceted characters made an emotional connection easy...."Janet, NetGalley Reviewer

Chapter One

"I HAVE TWO DAYS TO FIND A FIANCÉ." Ignoring the anxiety that tightened her stomach, Graceann Palmer dipped her fork into her apple pie à la mode and slipped the tasty treat into her mouth.

Her friend Kate sat next to her at the counter in the quaint fifties-era Spirit Lake Diner, located just outside the small Pennsylvania town of the same name. Kate grinned. "You could advertise online: *Fiancé wanted for Christmas. Good pay. Temporary position.*"

"Like I'd get a real upstanding guy that way," Graceann said.

Kate shot her a sympathetic smile. "Face it. You'll have to tell your family you lied."

Bing Crosby's *I'll Be Home for Christmas* flowed from the jukebox, mocking Graceann. Her lie had caught up with her. She would come home for Christmas, minus a made-up fiancé.

Graceann finished her pie and pushed the plate away. "Tell my family the truth and have my mom try to fix me up with someone like the dentist she invited to spend the holidays with us last year? Boring, conceited, and he couldn't keep his hands to himself. Yuck."

The door opened, bringing in a fresh round of cold, snowy late December air. Shivering, Graceann drew her sweater closer around her.

"I wouldn't mind finding *that* under my Christmas tree," Kate said.

Graceann followed her friend's gaze to the tall man who'd just entered the diner. Dressed all in black—black motorcycle boots, black jeans, black leather jacket—and walking with the lithe grace of a panther, he took a seat at the other end of the counter. She studied him while he studied the menu. He had classic "bad boy" written all over his features—sharp cheekbones, dark stubble on a square jaw, and midnight black hair tied into a ponytail. Long, tapered fingers held the menu.

Suddenly, he looked up. Clear blue eyes connected with hers. Recognition spiked through her and sent her pulse jumping like a kid on Christmas morning.

"The Falcon," she whispered.

"What?" Kate gasped. "You're right. It *is* The Falcon."

His full lips tilted in a slow, sexy grin, showing even white teeth. He nodded at them before turning his attention to the waitress. After he gave his order, he didn't look in their direction again.

Kate gripped Graceann's arm, her fingers digging into Graceann's flesh beneath the heavy sweater. "Wow. The Falcon. I heard he left town the day after his graduation from Spirit Lake High fourteen years ago and hasn't been heard from since."

"Wonder what he's doing back here," Graceann said. In school, she'd had a crush on The Falcon even though he was two years ahead of her. She'd never told anyone, not even Kate.

"He's a little scruffy," Kate said.

"Scruffy, my tush. He's hot."

Kate grabbed her arm again as Graceann lifted her coffee mug. Coffee sloshed over the sides onto the counter. Setting the mug down, Graceann gave her friend an exasperated look. "What?"

"I have it," Kate said. "Your fiancé."

"What are you talking about?"

"The Falcon. I'll bet he'll pretend to be your fiancé. After Zach bowed out, you said you'd be willing to pay someone. The Falcon always needed cash. Do it. Ask him."

"You're crazy. I haven't seen him in fourteen years. He could be a serial killer for all we know."

Kate shook her head. "He's not. We would have heard." She leaned closer. "You'll be at your grandmother's with the whole family. You'll be safe. Your grandmother is old-fashioned. She'll put you in separate rooms. It's not like he's a total stranger. Bring him to meet the family, pretend you're wildly in love. Your mom will quit trying to fix you up. After the holidays you won't ever have to see him again. Once you're back in New York, you can tell your family you broke the engagement. That's what you planned to do with Zach."

Graceann put a hand up. "This is the craziest idea you've ever had, and you've had plenty. I can't ask this guy to go along with my scheme. I'll have to resign myself to fending off another loser my mom pushes at me. She means well, but she won't accept that I'm not interested in marriage. After what Michael did, my whole family feels sorry for me. I don't want or need their pity."

"Michael was a jerk. He didn't deserve you. Listen to me, Graceann. Ask. The. Falcon. What could it hurt to at least ask?"

"His name is Jake, and I'll think about it."

"Don't wait too long. He'll be out of here and you'll have missed your chance."

Graceann sipped her coffee and stole glances at Jake Falco. Maybe Kate was right. Jake had always been nice to her and had even come to her aid once when the mean girls were harassing her. He might help her out now. At her grandmother's, they'd be surrounded by family. She wouldn't be alone with him. Her gut feelings were usually on target, so she'd learned to listen. She'd ignored her instincts with Michael and look how that had turned out. Something was telling her to go ahead and take a chance on Jake.

"I'll do it." She stood before she lost her nerve.

He raised his head as she approached. His eyes, blue as a bright winter sky, lit with awareness. He brazenly scanned her in the same way he used to check out some of the other girls in school, but never her.

Her heart pounded, the sound pulsing in her ears. She nearly turned to rush back to her stool, but desperation propelled her toward him.

"Graceann Palmer," he said when she reached him. His voice, deep, smoky, richer than she remembered, warmed her like well-aged whiskey.

The opening line she'd rehearsed dried in her throat. "Hello, Fal…Jake," she stammered.

He gestured to the stool next to him and threw her a sardonic smile. "Have a seat. Catch up on old times."

What was she doing? They were no longer in high school. This man was a stranger to her now. She sat down gingerly and glanced over at Kate. Her friend gave her the thumbs-up sign.

"So, Graceann Palmer," he said, turning in his stool to face her. "What have you been up to?"

Giddily flattered that he remembered her name, she found the words to answer him. "I moved to

New York City." She smoothed a hand over her jeans, feeling as nervous as the awkward teen she'd once been. "I design jewelry."

He quirked an eyebrow. "Impressive. Did you design that necklace you're wearing?"

She raised her left hand to rub the large blue stone set in sterling silver and hanging from a silver chain. It was one of her favorites. "I did."

Uneasy under his intense gaze, she lowered her hand to rest it on her thigh.

"Not married?" he asked.

Her chest knotted with the familiar pain of betrayal. "Not married. What about you?"

"Nope. Never been."

Whew. She hadn't considered the possibility he'd be married. "Where do you live and what sort of work do you do?"

"I live here and there," he said with a shrug. "Some would say I don't work at all."

"Intriguing." She noted the age and well-worn dullness of his distressed leather jacket. Maybe Kate was right. He'd lived on the poor side of town when they were growing up. Maybe things hadn't improved since he'd lit out all those years ago.

The sounds of food sizzling on the griddle and silver clanking against glass filled the diner, but an uncomfortable silence settled between them. The pungent odor of hamburger and onions cooking roiled her already unsettled stomach.

"I'm surprised you recognized me," she said into the silence. "It's been fourteen years."

He studied her. When his glance dropped to her mouth, his eyes darkened. "How could I forget those beautiful green cat eyes of yours or those lips?" he said in a husky voice.

Stunned silent, she opened her mouth and snapped it shut. Up close, he carried the scent and the appearance of the outdoors—all hard muscles, bronzed skin and the aroma of clean, pine-scented air. She swallowed. It was easy to believe the rumors that had swirled around him in school, stories about the women he'd slept with. Not girls. Women. He was playing with her. He couldn't really be trying to seduce her. Unlike the insecure girl she'd been, she could now handle the likes of Jake Falco.

Graceann drew a deep breath and plunged in. "I have a proposition for you."

He quirked that eyebrow again. "Sounds interesting."

"It's not what you think."

He laughed. "What I'm thinking is very good."

Heat suffused her cheeks. "Clean out your mind. It's a business proposition."

"Too bad." He signaled the waitress for two cups of coffee, then re-settled onto his stool, his attention on Graceann. "Go on. I'm listening."

Covering her anxiety, she added cream to her coffee, stirred, then took too big a sip and choked as the liquid burned its way down her throat.

11

He patted her on her back until she waved him away. "I'm fine," she managed. Pushing aside her cup to let the drink cool, she locked her gaze with his. She would not let him intimidate her.

"I need a fiancé."

His lips tilted in amusement. "Are you asking me to marry you, Ms. Palmer?"

"No. I'm asking you to pretend we're engaged."

He lowered his gaze, stared into his coffee, then back to her. "Why would I do that?"

"I'll pay you five thousand dollars."

His features tightened. "You think I need money?"

"No! I'm the one who's desperate."

"I see." He smiled, but the smile didn't touch his eyes.

"Wait. That didn't come out right. I'm desperate because my pretend fiancé canceled out on me at the last minute and I need a substitute. Fast."

"Baby, I'm not a substitution for any man."

"No, I didn't mean—"

"Forget it." He studied her for a moment, then smiled thoughtfully and reached out to brush a strand of her hair off her face. His touch sent heat flowing like warmed honey through her veins. "Just know I'm the real thing, princess."

She pulled away. "Stop playing with me. This is strictly business. You come with me to my grandmother's house day after tomorrow.

We stay through the holidays. We pretend we're in love. Everyone is happy. New Year's Day I pay you the five thousand. We go our separate ways."

Turning away, he sipped his coffee. Then he put down his cup and met her gaze. "Why would you need a fake fiancé? I would think you could have as many men as you wanted."

"Why is my business. What do you say? Or do you already have Christmas plans?"

A shadow seemed to flit across his face. "I have no plans."

She bit down on her lip. "Well?"

He glanced at her left hand again. "We'll need a ring."

Relief flooded her. *Yes!* He'd do it. She was safe from another terrible fix-up. "I made a ring. It's cubic zirconia, but it looks like the real thing."

He laughed. "You come prepared."

"A friend was going to act the part of my fiancé, but at the last minute he got an invitation to go to Santo Domingo with his new girlfriend."

"Not much of a friend."

"Zach would have stayed, but I told him not to worry about me. He really likes this new girl and I didn't want to wreck it for him. Zach had his heart broken a year ago and needs someone in his life."

"You're a good friend as well as beautiful." Giving her another of his sexy grins, he held out his hand to shake hers. "Well, Ms. Graceann Palmer, it's a deal. You've hired yourself a fiancé."

Chapter Two

JAKE SHIFTED HIS GARMENT BAG to his other hand and picked up his duffel when the dark blue BMW with Graceann at the wheel drove into the parking lot of the Spirit Lake Diner. She pulled up and gave him a tentative smile. If possible, she was sexier than she was two days ago when he'd agreed to go along with her crazy plan. He had his reasons for agreeing to help her, but he wouldn't delve into them now.

He walked around to the passenger side, opened the back door, deposited his duffel on the floor, hung the garment bag, then got into the front seat. "A punctual woman," he said as he fastened his seatbelt. "First woman I've known to do that."

She pulled out of the parking lot and slid a glance at him. "How many women have you known?"

He chuckled at the way her face reddened. For all her innate sexuality, she still retained the innocence he remembered from all those years ago. "I've known a few."

"I'll bet you have."

"Are you being sarcastic, Ms. Palmer?"

"No, not at all. I'm sorry. I'm really grateful to you for helping me out like this."

He didn't want her gratitude. A kiss? He wouldn't refuse that, though. "Nice car," he said.

"It belongs to Zach. I don't own a car. Don't need one in New York City." She cleared her throat. "When we get close to my grandmother's I'll pull over and we can change places. They know I don't have a car so we'll tell them this is yours."

He shrugged. "Whatever." He settled into his seat and watched the countryside flash by like a Currier & Ives winter scene. The Poconos were beautiful this time of year with snow blanketing the mountains. There'd been times in the past fourteen years when he'd actually missed it here.

Between Christmas and New Year's the place would be swarming with skiers. He'd never been part of the ski crowd, never been part of any crowd. Suited him just fine. He studied Graceann's profile. Her straight nose and firm chin hinted at a strength he suspected she didn't know she had. Concentrating on her driving, she flicked out her tongue to sweep along her top lip.

He shifted as his jeans got a little tighter. He wondered if she realized how damn sexy she was. She must have felt him watching because she glanced at him. "What are you looking at?"

"You, and it's a beautiful sight."

Her attention back on the winding road, she said, "Stop playing, Jake."

"Aren't we supposed to be in love? I'm in fiancé mode already."

"Save it for the family."

"Why don't you tell me what's going on? The truth. Since you hired me, I think I need to know why you're doing this and what I'm up against."

She gripped the steering wheel with her gloved hands and concentrated on the road. "It's like this. My mother thinks I need a man in my life. I've told her I'm not interested in marriage, but she won't believe me. Especially after what happened two years ago."

"What happened?"

She turned those big green eyes on him for a second, then focused back on the road. "I was in a relationship. He wasn't who I thought he was. It ended badly."

A twinge of guilt made Jake shift uneasily. He wasn't exactly who Graceann thought he was either.

"Anyway," she continued. "My family feels sorry for me. They were upset by what happened. My sister has a terrific husband and two wonderful kids, my parents have had a happy marriage for almost forty years. They, especially my mother, won't rest until I'm safely married."

"How is having a temporary fiancé going to help things? When the holidays are over, we go our separate ways."

"I'll tell them I broke the engagement. If they think I broke up with you, they'll stop feeling sorry for me because they'll know I'm in control of my life and perfectly happy on my own."

He sank into his seat, making himself more comfortable. "There's a flaw in your plan. I don't believe your family will let up on you. Are you going to hire a new fiancé every Christmas?"

She laughed, a clear, crystal sound that floated through the car and arrowed straight to the empty places in his heart.

"I know my family. My plan will work."

"Let's hope so. For your sake. Tell me about your family."

She visibly relaxed and he guessed she was more at ease talking about a safer subject.

"My dad is Mark," she began. "He's a retired engineer. He owned his own engineering firm. My mom is Angie. She, along with two friends, used to own a gift shop in town. My sister is Lorrie, a schoolteacher, but now a stay-at-home mom. She's six years older than I am so she was out of school when you started. Her husband is Andrew. He works for an insurance company. And there's Grandmom." Graceann's voice softened. "I grew up in Grandmom's house. We all lived with her. My parents still do. Grandmom's the greatest."

At her obvious love for her family, a familiar knot of regret and loss tightened in Jake's chest. He shoved it away, back deep inside him where it belonged.

A half hour later Graceann turned off the main road onto a smaller road, then pulled over. He recognized it as the driveway to Spirit Manor, the Palmer family mansion. Once, as a teenager, he'd taken his newly-restored motorcycle out for a test drive. Harry, the mechanic he did odd jobs for all through school, had given him the wreck of a bike two years before. Jake had lovingly restored it, and on a glorious spring day he'd ridden it to the outskirts of town where the wealthy people lived. He'd driven up to Spirit Manor to get a glimpse of Graceann's house. He still remembered the feeling of sitting on his bike and gazing at the large stone mansion, wondering what it would feel like to have a real family, with siblings, and loving parents.

He'd done all right for himself. The good people of Spirit Lake might have ignored him and brushed him aside as Falco trash, but that was their problem. Revenge was a bitch.

He and Graceann exchanged places, and he adjusted the seat and mirrors, put the car in gear and drove the rest of the way. The house, gray stone with a turret on one side, loomed ahead, peeking through the evergreens like an ancient ever-watchful sentinel. Jake rubbed his hand along his denim-clad thigh as anxiety wound through him. He shouldn't be nervous. He was only playing a part, something he was good at. He'd been acting, hiding his true self, for most of his life.

He pulled into the circular driveway in front of the impressive structure. The sculptured fountain with its marble carving of an Ancient Roman woman surrounded by fish spewing water was now covered and dry. He remembered admiring the fountain that long-ago spring day. The statue with her arms outstretched seemed to welcome all visitors. He'd wondered then if the flesh and blood family would welcome him as the marble woman seemed to. Would they welcome him now?

Next to him, Graceann let out a sigh. "Here we are. Curtain time."

He unfastened his seatbelt and leaned toward her. "Might as well start now." Framing her face between his hands, he touched his lips to hers. At first she stiffened, but he continued to press his lips against hers, drinking in her sweetness. Her lips softened and she let out a low moan. Surprised and pleased at her reaction, he deepened the kiss, slipping his tongue into her willing mouth. She slid her hands up his chest and pressed closer.

Suppressing a groan, he fought the desire to skim his hands over her ribcage to her chest. For a petite woman, she had magnificent breasts.

The sound of voices cut through his sensual haze. He reluctantly drew away. Graceann watched him with wonder in her incredible eyes. Her breathing was labored. He resisted a smile. This gig might be lots more interesting than he'd hoped.

"That was for practice, right?" She rubbed a finger over her lips and lowered her voice. "You really know how to play a part."

"You didn't like it?"

Her face pinked. "It doesn't matter what I like. This is a business deal."

"So you keep reminding me." He looked toward the steps where a group of people huddled watching them. "Your family?"

She looked over and groaned. "Do you think they saw us?"

"I'm sure they did. You stay there and I'll come around and open your door."

"I'm capable of opening my own door."

He touched the tip of her nose. "But we want to make a good impression, especially on your grandmother."

"Then maybe we'd better sit here for a little while," she said with a pointed glance at his lap.

He grinned. "See what you do to me?" When she rolled her eyes, he laughed. "Give me a minute or two."

"I'll get out first." She unfastened her seatbelt, opened the car door, and stepped out. With a wave to the group on the steps, she called out, "Hey, everybody. We're here."

Jake watched as her family ran down the steps to greet her. His lips still burned from their kiss. Damn! The woman could kiss.

After she'd been hugged by each member of her family, they looked toward him, and Jake knew it was show time. He looked down. Good to go. With a grimace, he left the car and walked toward the group. Graceann grabbed his hand and drew him forward. "Everyone, this is Jake Falco, my fiancé."

He could swear he heard a note of pride in her voice. He dismissed it as wishful thinking.

"Jake, this is my grandmother, Bea Palmer," she said, indicating a slender woman in her eighties with softly curling blonde hair and a twinkle in her blue eyes.

"So happy to meet you, Jake," her grandmother said, holding out her hand.

He took her hand, noting how fragile it felt, like a small bird. "Nice to meet you, Mrs. Palmer."

"Call me Grandmom."

In a rush, Graceann introduced him to her mother Angie, an older version of Graceann, who shook his hand and frowned. "Falco? Are you from around here?"

"Jake's from Brooklyn," Graceann said.

She quickly introduced him to the rest of the family—her dad Mark, who gave him a tight smile while he assessed Jake. Her sister Lorrie, a blonde who resembled their father, gave him a quick hug. Next came Lorrie's husband Andrew, a slim balding man, and their two kids, baby Christian and toddler Isabella. Jake's head swam with all the names. The love the Palmer family had for each other was palpable, filling the air. A pang of envy for all he'd missed tugged at his heart.

"Let's see the ring," Lorrie said, diverting his attention.

Graceann slipped off one black leather glove and held out her left hand. A huge stone glimmered in the weak sunlight. Smaller stones surrounded the main one. Graceann was a hell of a jewelry designer. He'd seen plenty of diamonds in his line of work, and if he didn't know any different, he'd think hers was the real deal.

The women gathered around ooohing and aaahing. Graceann's father looked at Jake and shrugged. Jake smiled.

"Let's go in," her dad said. When Jake moved to go to the car to get their luggage, her dad shooed him away, saying, "We'll get that later."

Graceann reached for Jake's hand as they climbed the marble steps. He leaned in to whisper in her ear. "Great ring. Could have fooled me."

"Thanks," she whispered. "Ready? Too late to back out now."

He squeezed her hand. "I'm not going anywhere."

Chapter Three

GRACEANN STEPPED INTO her grandmother's large marble-floored foyer. Inhaling the sweetly sharp aroma of holly and evergreens, she glanced around, trying to picture the festively decorated space through Jake's eyes. The oversized potted poinsettia plants around the perimeter showcased the stately Christmas tree, lit by a myriad of twinkling white lights and festooned with multi-colored balls. The tree stood in the niche formed by the curving staircase and stretched from the floor to almost touch the two-story high ceiling. Memories of happy family Christmases flooded her, warming her all over.

But more was happening to her than joyous holiday memories. Jake's hand in hers had tingles running up her arm. And that kiss in the car even now warmed her like hundreds of burning Christmas candles. Maybe she'd made a mistake in hiring him as her pretend fiancé. It would take all her willpower to get through the holidays without wanting another kiss.

At least.

She stared at Jake, but couldn't read his expression. Vaguely disappointed he didn't seem to share her enthusiasm for the beautiful holiday decor, she forced a smile and turned to her grandmother. "Grandmom, the tree's more beautiful than usual, if possible."

"Thank you, dear. Your mother and Lorrie did most of it."

"I love it."

"We guys carried the tree in and set it up," Andrew, Lorrie's husband, said.

Lorrie patted his hand. "Of course you did."

Graceann laughed, letting go some of her tension.

"It is beautiful, Mrs. Palmer," Jake said at last, with a smile for the older woman.

"How nice of you to say, Jake. But please call me Grandmom." She touched Graceann's arm. "Let's go into the dining room. We're having a casual lunch."

The family moved almost as one toward the dining room at the right of the foyer. Graceann released Jake's hand and followed the others. Not hearing him behind her, she turned around.

He stood very still staring at the tree.

"Jake?"

He turned to her and blinked. Longing flashed in his eyes so quickly she wondered if she imagined it.

"We're having lunch now," she said.

He swept his arm out. "After you, princess."

Before he could take a step, the sound of barking, then the click of nails on the hardwood stairs heralded the arrival of her grandmother's Shih Tzu, Fluffy. Yapping loudly the dog ran right at Jake.

Jake stepped away from the animal. Fluffy continued yapping and running around Jake's feet.

"It's only Fluffy," Graceann said. "He won't hurt you."

"That's what they all say," he ground out. "I prefer cats."

Graceann widened her eyes. "You have cats? That's good to know in case anyone in the family asks."

He nodded and again tried to sidestep Fluffy. "I have two."

"Where are they?"

"With a friend."

"Fluffy, come in here," her grandmother called.

Jake let out an audible breath as the dog trotted into the dining room. "Let's eat," he said.

Frowning, Graceann led him into the other room where a table that could easily seat one dozen was set for lunch.

Jake leaned over to whisper in Graceann's ear. "This is a casual lunch? Is the whole town dropping by to eat?"

"This is Grandmom's idea of an informal meal," she whispered back.

When they were settled at the table laden with bowls of Greek salad and plates of cheese soufflé, along with baskets of crusty French bread, Jake picked up his fork and dipped it into his salad. Graceann, seated next to him, touched his arm.

He gave her a quizzical look, and she said, "We have to say grace."

"Sorry." He put down his fork.

"Mark," her grandmother said, with a nod toward Graceann's father.

The family bowed their heads. Graceann watched Jake through lowered lashes. He had bowed his head, too. He was trying to fit in. Good. Maybe things would work out.

"Lord, thank you for this food, and thank you for bringing Jake into our household and into Graceann's life. Now, dig in." Her dad winked at her.

She grabbed her water goblet and gulped, wishing she could wash away the guilt of deceiving her family as easily as she washed away the dryness in her throat. She hated lying to them.

After lunch, Jake brought their bags from the car. Graceann deposited hers in her room, then showed Jake to his room. She smiled as they headed to the other end of the long hallway. Leave it to Grandmom to put them as far apart as possible. As if a hallway would stop them if she and Jake were truly lovers.

"Here we are," she said when they'd reached the guest room where Jake would spend the next nine days. She swung the door open. Carrying his garment bag and duffel, he followed her.

"Nice." His gaze swept the large room, done in various shades of blue. A queen-sized bed covered in a navy blue comforter was set against the far wall under windows that looked out to the lake. Jake set his bags on the bed and moved the white curtains aside to peer out. "Great view. As a kid, I always wondered what it would be like to live here."

"You did?"

He turned from the windows. "Silly, huh?" He scanned her, and his eyes flashed with desire. "Maybe I just wondered what it would be like to be close to you."

He'd taken off his leather jacket, and the deep blue sweater he wore made his eyes bluer and emphasized the broadness of his muscled chest. His faded jeans hugged legs that went on forever. She wondered if he worked out, then licked her lips at the delicious image of Jake pumping iron.

"We're alone now," she said. "You can drop the act."

"Oh?" He stalked toward her, a predator after his prey. When he reached her, he touched her chin with his index finger, tilting her head until their eyes met. An unexpected sensual tension flared between them. "Maybe it's not an act."

Graceann forgot how to breathe.

Jake smiled and leaned in for a kiss.

Graceann lifted her hands instinctively to put space between them. "Jake. No. Really. I, uh—"

A furious yapping broke the moment. Jake stepped back, away from Fluffy's teeth snapping too close to Jake's ankles. "What is the matter with that dog?"

"He knows you don't like him." She suppressed a laugh at the sight of the tall, muscled Jake and the tiny barking dog. Or was it a laugh of relief?

"Down," he said to the little dog, who suddenly quieted and sat silently watching Jake. "This is why I like cats. They don't bother you."

Graceann couldn't hold her laughter any longer. When she finally composed herself she wiped away tears to find Jake staring at her, his features tight.

"You think it's funny this little monster keeps bothering me?"

She nodded. "I'm sorry, but it is."

His features relaxed and he chuckled "I guess so."

"Why don't you like dogs?"

"One bit me when I was ten. I had to go to the ER."

"That explains it." One mystery solved. "Would

you like me to speak to Grandmom and have her quarantine Fluffy for the duration?"

"No, I can deal with a yappy dog. But thanks."

Her gaze went to his bags on the bed. "You should unpack, then we can go downstairs to join the rest of the family. Okay?"

He grinned. "You're the boss. I'm only the hired gun."

She rolled her eyes, making him laugh.

He nodded toward the windows. "I saw the dock out there. After I unpack, how about we take a walk to the lake?"

He wanted to be alone with her? The thought thrilled and scared her. Unable to find words, she nodded.

Her grandmother's voice calling Fluffy drifted to them from downstairs. With one last yap at Jake, the dog bolted out of the room.

"I'm glad he's gone," Jake said.

"You and Fluffy have nine days to learn to tolerate each other." She frowned. "I think it's going well with the family, don't you?"

"I'm not sure. Your mother thought I seemed familiar."

"My family wouldn't know you. My parents barely knew the kids in my high school class. They didn't know any of the kids in the other classes. And my sister was four years ahead of you. I think our secret is safe."

"Our families weren't exactly in the same social circles either."

She wondered at the tinge of bitterness in his voice.

"We need to work out some details if we're going to carry this off." He sat on the bed and patted the spot next to him.

Graceann sank onto the bed, being careful to sit as far from him as possible. The mattress dipped, the movement sliding her a little closer to him than she thought prudent. Amusement glinted in Jake's eyes as he watched her. She folded her hands demurely on her lap, trying to ignore the clean, outdoors scent of him, the way the beginnings of a stubble on his square jaw gave him the look of a pirate. The way her heart pounded.

Jake's mouth tilted in a mocking grin. "Afraid of me, princess?"

"Not on your life." She scooched over a little, away from him. "What do you want to talk about?"

"Your family is going to have a lot more questions about me. You told them I live in Brooklyn. No way do I have a Brooklyn accent."

She smoothed a hand over her jeans, gathering her thoughts. "I know. It was the first thing I could think of. Zach's from Brooklyn."

"You worked it all out with Zach, but not me? Never mind. Let's use Zach's information. What type of work does he do?"

"What do you do? We'll use that."

He shook his head. "We'll use Zach's."

She wondered if Jake was into something illegal. Her stomach churned at the thought. "Zach is a trader with a Wall Street firm," she said slowly.

Jake laughed. "I don't look like anyone's idea of a Wall Street trader."

She glanced down at his motorcycle boots. "I know. We'll say you repair and customize motorcycles."

"That'll work. When I was in school I restored an old motorcycle. Still have the thing. Do you think your parents will be happy their little princess is with a mechanic?"

"Stop calling me princess. You're over thinking everything. Just play the part."

He stood. "At least your parents will be relieved when you tell them you broke the engagement."

She stood, too. "My parents will accept any man I love if they think the guy will treat me right. They're not snobby."

He turned away from her. "I need to unpack." He unzipped his duffel and began to pull out T-shirts and sweaters. Going to the large dresser, he opened drawers and carefully set the garments inside.

With a glance at Graceann, he said, "I don't need help, but if you want to give me a hand, suit yourself." He nodded toward the garment bag.

Still musing over the abrupt change in conversation,

Graceann grabbed the bag, hung it in the closet and began to empty it. Thoughtfully, she ran a hand over a white Egyptian cotton shirt with a designer label, then unpacked several other similar shirts in different colors, four pairs of black slacks, and several pairs of expensive jeans. When she pulled out a beautifully tailored gray suit sporting the label of a top designer, she blinked. A pricey collection for a man who didn't own up to having a regular job.

"Nice clothes," she said when she'd finished hanging them in the walk-in closet.

"I have a taste for the finer things."

"Where do you live, Jake?"

"Wherever it suits me." He didn't look at her.

"What about your cats?"

He turned to her with a cocky grin. "In good hands. Don't worry about them, princess."

Instead, the mischievous look he gave her told her she should be worried about *him*.

Chapter Four

AFTER JAKE UNPACKED, he and Graceann strolled along the wooden walkway to the dock behind her grandmother's house. Shivering with the cold, he dug his hands into the pockets of his leather jacket and inhaled the clean, crisp air, redolent with the scent of pine. His jacket wasn't heavy enough, but he'd been away so long he'd forgotten how brutal the winters could be here in the Poconos.

He glanced over at Graceann, walking next to him and bundled into a wool jacket, scarf and gloves. Their breaths mingled in the frosty air, a reminder of the kiss they would have shared in the bedroom if that pesky little dog hadn't appeared.

Graceann gave him a shaky smile. He made her nervous. Good. It meant she wasn't immune to him. Why that suddenly mattered he had no idea.

Reaching out, he took her hand. When she tried to pull away, he gripped it tighter and leaned over to whisper in her ear. "You never know who might be watching from the house. We have to put on a convincing show."

"All right, but don't take advantage of the situation."

"Who me? Take advantage?"

She laughed. The sound made his heart jump. He liked seeing her smile and hearing her laugh. Her carefree response shed a soft light into the dark places returning to Spirit Lake had reopened.

When they got to the dock, still holding hands, they stared out over the ice-crusted lake. "I used to love coming to the lake when I was a kid," he said. "Any troubles I had dissolved into the water, regardless of the time of year."

"What kind of troubles?" She looked up at him with luminous green eyes that reminded him of a brightly shining Christmas light. Calm, clear, innocent eyes. The kind that could look into and steal a man's soul.

He shrugged. "The usual kid stuff. Nothing serious." *Liar.*

She studied him before turning to gaze out over the water again. "It is pretty here. I miss it at times. In the summer I usually go to the Hamptons on weekends. Zach has a house there. But sometimes I come home and hang out here."

An unexpected stab of jealousy knifed Jake. "You and this Zach, you're close?"

With a nod, she turned back to him. "He and Kate are my best friends. Kate lives here but she comes up to New York to stay with me whenever she can. I usually stay with my parents when I come back, but I've been staying at Kate's place nearby the last few days. We wanted some girl time. Now that she has a boyfriend, I don't see her as much."

"You and Zach, were you ever...did you ever...?" He knew he sounded like an idiot, but he had to know.

"God, no. He's more like a brother to me. He lived in the apartment next door when I first moved to New York. He was a big help, showing me around the city. Why do you ask?"

He shrugged. He couldn't explain what he didn't understand himself, but the thought of her with another man clenched his gut.

"Zach was going to pretend to be your fiancé?" he asked. "Don't your parents know him?"

"They never met him. The few times they came to New York to see me, Zach was away. That's why he would have been perfect as my fiancé, but I think you'll work out just fine," she said with a smile.

Returning her smile, he slid his arm around her

waist and pulled her against him. When she started to protest, he said, "Our audience, remember?"

"Now I know you're taking advantage of the situation."

"Always. But you're paying me and I always give my customers their money's worth."

Quiet, she stared out over the lake again, but didn't pull away.

"Why doesn't a woman like you have a boyfriend or a husband?" he asked.

She lifted a wide-eyed gaze to his. "What do you mean, a woman like me?"

"Smart, sexy, stunning. I should think you'd be fighting the men off."

She swallowed. "Me? Stunning?"

"You don't see it, do you?"

"Let's drop that line of conversation. You can tell *me* something though."

"Maybe."

"Did you like being called The Falcon?"

"Sometimes." Graceann came from a loving, supportive family. She wouldn't understand the ugliness and shame of his upbringing.

"Does anyone call you that now?"

"Nope." Forcing a smile, he tried to relax and turned his attention back to the still lake.

"Not real forthcoming with information, are you?"

"Depends on who's asking."

"Are your parents still alive?" she asked.

He stiffened. "They died a few years ago, within months of each other. They were living in Florida."

"I'm sorry to hear that. They couldn't have been more than—fifty or so? Was it an accident? Were they in the hospital?"

He felt the weight of her curiosity, but continued to stare out over the lake. "No." He wasn't about to tell her the sordid details of their passing.

An owl hooted in the wind, making him shiver inside.

"You must be freezing in that coat," she said, so gently it nearly ripped a hole in his hardened heart. "Let's go back in," she said quietly. "I could use a cup of hot chocolate."

Grateful beyond words that she hadn't pursued the subject, he followed her into the house, his thoughts a tumble. Somehow he had to change his game plan, find a way to keep Graceann off-guard so she wouldn't ask so many questions.

Later that day, Graceann, her mother and her sister worked together in the kitchen preparing dinner. Her grandmother had given her cook and housekeeper time off so they could spend the holidays with their own families.

The other adults sat in the adjacent great room talking, watching a football game, drinking, and nibbling on appetizers. Tomorrow was Christmas Eve and the house would be a bustle of activity for a few days, but today was laid-back, a time to chill out.

"How did you and Jake meet? You've been so secretive about him." Her sister Lorrie glanced at Graceann then went back to slicing vegetables for the salad.

Their mother slid the chicken breasts into the oven, then washed her hands.

Graceann looked around the large white recently renovated kitchen that opened into the great room, or family room, before turning her attention to her mother and sister. "Why are we in here cooking while the men sit around? What is this, the nineteenth century?"

"Stop trying to change the subject." Lorrie pinned Graceann with her eyes. "How did you and Jake meet?"

"I want to know, too." Her mother grabbed a stool next to the center island and settled onto it. She reached out and plucked a few grape tomatoes from the dish in front of Lorrie and popped one into her mouth.

Graceann set down the paring knife she was using to peel the potatoes. She inhaled the tangy scents of lemon and rosemary rising from the chicken. The signature cinnamon cake Grandmom had baked earlier cooled on the counter. Its aroma mingled with the lemon and rosemary, sweetening the air.

"We met at the Hamptons this past May. Jake's friends owned a house next to my friend Zach's." The lie rolled easily, too easily, off her tongue. A knot of guilt and anxiety tightened in her chest. She hoped her dad hadn't asked Jake the same question. Desperate, she really hadn't thought this whole thing through before presenting Jake with her proposition.

Lorrie set down her own knife. "Hamptons, huh? Jake doesn't look like the Hamptons type." She grinned. "He sure is sexy though."

"Lorrie, you're a married woman and a mother," their mom said.

"Please, Mom." Lorrie rolled her eyes. "Like you never noticed any good-looking guys after you met Daddy."

Shaking her head, Graceann went back to peeling the potatoes.

"Despite his long hair and that black leather, Jake seems nice enough," her mother said.

The tone in her voice made Graceann stop peeling and wait for the "but" she knew would come.

"But," her mom continued, "he repairs motorcycles? With your education and your background, are you sure he's the man you want to spend your life with?"

Graceann dropped her paring knife. It clanked onto the granite counter. "Mom, you sound so snobby. That's not like you."

"Seriously, Graceann," Lorrie said. "Hunky as he is, Jake's a little rough around the edges. Not your type at all."

Graceann gripped the edge of the counter. "Remember how you all loved Michael, the Wall Street wizard with the fancy car and clothes, the penthouse in Manhattan? How'd he turn out?" She could feel her temper rising. "A snazzy resume and a lot of stuff don't make a guy my type. Besides, how do you know what my type is?"

"Wow, we hit a nerve," Lorrie said.

"We're not being snobs, dear." Her mom reached across the counter and touched Graceann's hand. "We only want you to be happy."

"I am happy."

Lorrie went back to her slicing. "Well, it's obvious you and Jake are in love, but...I just hope it all works out for you."

Graceann stilled. She and Jake in love? They weren't *that* good at acting. Trying to digest Lorrie's words, she went back to peeling potatoes.

Her mother cleared her throat. "I saw Steven Craig a few weeks ago."

"I haven't seen Steven in years," Graceann said, concentrating on peeling and chopping. "How is he?"

"He left Philadelphia. Didn't like the city. He's decided to stay on the East Coast. He said he liked it here in the Poconos the times he visited with you so he's setting up a law office nearby in Harmony and bought a house there. He asked about you, and even gave me his phone number to give to you."

"Nice to know he's doing well, but I'm not interested in calling him." Finished with the potatoes, Graceann walked over to the cabinets and pulled out a large pot, then went to the sink and began filling the pot with water.

"I always liked Steven and hoped you and he would get together permanently some day," her mother said.

Her mind only half on what her mother was saying, Graceann continued to fill the pot. "Steven and I dated off-and-on those two years in college. We parted friends."

"He's spending the holidays alone. His parents are in Europe."

The implication behind her mother's words penetrated Graceann's brain. A shiver of apprehension, cold as the water streaming into the pot, ran up her spine. She set down the pot, turned off the faucet and faced her mother.

"Mom, what are you trying to say?" Graceann pressed back against the hard edge of the sink. Maybe it would give her strength for what she feared her mother was about to admit.

Her mom fidgeted, then, with a sheepish grin, said, "I invited him to spend Christmas with us and stay for a few days."

"You didn't!"

"Really, Mom," Lorrie said. "This is a family Christmas and Graceann brought her new fiancé. How do you think Jake will feel when one of Graceann's old boyfriends shows up?"

Graceann threw her sister a smile of gratitude, then turned to her mother. "You knew I was bringing someone home. Why did you invite Steven? When did you invite him?"

"You said you were dating someone," her mother said, a note of exasperation in her voice. "Suddenly you're engaged. I'd already invited Steven."

"Lorrie's right. Everyone will be uncomfortable. Un-invite Steven."

Her mother stood, a stubborn look Graceann recognized all too well on her face. "I will not un-invite Steven. That's very uncharitable of both of you. The poor man was planning to spend Christmas alone. He's an old friend. Inviting him was the least I could do. I'm sure Graceann and Jake will handle it."

Graceann stared at the ceiling in frustration. Things were bad enough with her trying to pass Jake off as her fiancé. Now Steven, who'd at one time begged Graceann to marry him, would be their guest. This time, her matchmaking mama had gone too far.

Chapter Five

MARK PALMER STROLLED INTO the kitchen. "How's everything going in here? Do you need any help?" Frowning, he glanced from one woman to the other.

"We're fine, Dad." Lorrie's words broke the tension that hovered in the air.

"I came in for beer for me and Andrew and a club soda for Jake." He turned to Graceann. "Is Jake a recovering alcoholic?"

Hell if I know. She almost blurted the words out loud. "Why do you ask?"

Her dad shrugged. "He said he didn't drink. Young men these days usually drink too much, if you ask me."

Graceann struggled to keep the surprise from registering on her face. She wouldn't have taken

Jake Falco, The Falcon, for a non-drinker. The guys he'd hung out with at school were reputed to be big partiers, but she hadn't known Jake well and didn't know if he drank. Maybe he'd given up drinking since then. "He's not a recovering alcoholic." She crossed her fingers behind her back and hoped she was telling the truth. "He just doesn't like alcohol."

"Strange." Her dad walked to the large stainless side-by-side refrigerator and pulled out two bottles of beer. "I'll be back for the club soda in a minute."

"I'll bring in the soda," Graceann said.

As he started to exit the room, he turned around and chuckled. "Isabella and Fluffy are both taken with your fiancé."

Some of her tension dissipated, and Graceann laughed. "Isabella and Fluffy the wonder dog? This I have to see."

When her father left the room, Lorrie grabbed Graceann's arm, stopping her on her way to the refrigerator.

"Why didn't you tell us Jake's name or anything about him before you got here? All you'd ever say is you were dating someone. What are you hiding?"

Graceann forced a smile. "I'm not hiding anything. We had a whirlwind romance, and we've just gotten engaged. I'm still trying to get used to the idea. I wanted to keep him my secret a little longer. And I was afraid if I told you too much about him,

I'd jinx our relationship. I talked constantly about Michael and look what happened." That excuse sounded lame even to her ears. She'd lied to them about dating someone, and she'd only hatched this crazy scheme with Zach three weeks ago. She wasn't even sure she'd have given them Zach's real name when he met them.

Anxious to escape the kitchen and the women's thoughtful gazes, she filled a glass with ice, poured a bottle of club soda over it, added a wedge of lime, and carried it to the other room.

The great room, comfortably furnished with two brown leather love seats and a matching sofa facing them, oversized tables and plush chairs, the hardwood floors covered with Oriental rugs, was her favorite room. A Christmas tree, smaller than the one in the entry hall, was set by the bay windows. The family would gather around that tree Christmas morning to open their gifts.

The picture that greeted her as she entered pushed aside her anger and anxiety about Steven. Jake was bouncing a laughing Isabella on his knee and Fluffy sat at his feet staring up at him. Jake might be a bit rough, he might be mysterious, but he had a way with children, and maybe dogs. He liked cats. There were reassuring depths to him she hadn't begun to fathom.

He looked up and their gazes caught. The air around them thickened. Andrew, Lorrie's husband, yelled at something on the TV, breaking the spell. Fluffy stood and barked at Jake. The sounds made baby Christian, asleep in his infant seat, stir, but he didn't waken.

"Here's your drink," she said to Jake. "I'll take Isabella."

She placed his drink on the table in front of him and he held out the toddler to her. Inhaling Isabella's sweet scent, she pressed the little girl close. Isabella's blonde curls tickled Graceann's face. She'd always wanted children, wanted it all—the loyal, faithful, loving husband, the house filled with laughter. Pets. But after Michael she didn't know if she could trust another man enough to open her heart.

Fluffy was in full yap mode now. Jake sipped his drink and warily watched the dog.

"Fluffy, leave that poor man alone and come over here," Grandmom said. With one last yap, Fluffy trotted over to Grandmom and settled at her feet.

Smiling, her grandmother looked toward Graceann. "Isabella looks good on you." With a pointed look at Jake, she said, "You and Jake will have beautiful children."

Jake choked on his drink. "I'm fine," he managed when Graceann started toward him. "Drink went down the wrong way." He wouldn't meet her gaze.

"Fluffy likes you, Jake," Grandmom said. "I've never seen my dog so fascinated with anyone."

"I'm not sure 'like' is the right word. I'm more of a cat person, and I think Fluffy knows it," Jake said.

"You and Graceann must get a dog and a cat after you're married," Grandmom said as if issuing a royal decree. She picked up a glass with her favorite drink, scotch on the rocks, and sipped, then looked at Graceann. "Will you live in New York?"

"We haven't decided yet," Graceann said quickly, catching Jake's eye.

"I will live anywhere Graceann wants," he put in amiably. "After all, my role in life is to make her happy."

Grandmom beamed. "How nice."

Her father and brother-in-law shot Jake incredulous looks.

The man was enjoying overplaying the devoted fiancé too much. Graceann intended to have a little talk with him later. She set down the squirming Isabella, who ran to her father. Then with a last warning look at Jake, Graceann went back to the kitchen.

Later that night, after the rest of the family had gone to bed, Graceann and Jake sat alone in the great room. A Hallmark Christmas movie played on TV. It was one Graceann had seen several times. "I love this movie," she said. "I'm a sucker for Christmas romance movies."

Jake slid his arm along the back of the love seat to her shoulders, then pulled her close. His muscled thigh pressed against hers and sent desire shooting through her. Although she found herself powerfully attracted to him, she tried to move away. Being this close to Jake was too emotionally dangerous.

He held her tighter. "Where do you think you're going?"

She turned to him, their faces a whisper apart. Words dried in her throat. She licked her lips. If she leaned forward even a little, she could kiss him. She straightened. "Everyone's in bed now. You can relax the act."

"What if someone has insomnia and decides to join us? We have to keep up appearances."

"Let's just watch the movie." She deliberately focused back on the TV, but barely registered what was on the screen. Jake was too darn distracting.

He chuckled but didn't release her. "I remember when this movie was shot. A friend of mine worked on it."

She turned to him. "You know someone in Hollywood? Really? Who?"

"No one you've ever heard of."

"Oh." Although she really would have liked to pursue the subject further, to delve into discovering Jake Falco, the man, she had to remind herself they had only a business deal. There was no need to get personal.

When the commercial came on, she pulled back and faced him. "We need to coordinate some things." *And I need to tell you my mother invited my ex-boyfriend to spend Christmas with us.*

He studied her with those cool, clear baby blues, making her shift uncomfortably. When he looked at her mouth, intention in his eyes, she scooted to the other end of the love seat.

"Do I make you nervous, Ms. Palmer?" Laughter tinged his voice.

"No."

"Liar."

"Let's talk business." She folded her arms across her chest.

"You're on."

"Did you tell anyone how we met?"

He shook his head. "Didn't come up."

"Here's the story. We met this past May in the Hamptons. I was staying at Zach's house and you were next door at a friend's. We'll call your friend Joe in case anyone asks. You and I have been together ever since."

"I don't have a friend named Joe." He shot her a wicked grin and slid closer. "At least I moved in on you fast." He took a strand of her hair and twirled it around his finger. "I like that. When I see what I want, I take it. I'd never wait too long to make you mine."

At his words, her pulse jumped. "Get serious."

"I am serious."

The man was an accomplished seducer. Yet, there'd been sincerity in his expression and his voice.

"Never mind that," she said. "That's our story and we're sticking to it."

He laughed softly.

She tilted her head and studied him. "Are you a recovering alcoholic?"

His features tightened as his lips thinned. "Why do you ask?"

"You don't drink."

Jake lowered his gaze and she thought he wouldn't answer. At last he turned to her with hooded eyes. "My parents drank enough for two lifetimes and lost their health before forty, their lives before fifty-five. I have no desire to be like them."

She touched his hand where it rested on the cushion. "I'm sorry, Jake. I didn't know."

He grasped her hand, holding it tight. Longing flared up deep inside her. The glow from the TV and the table lamp cast a pale light that emphasized his sculpted cheekbones and full lips. She wanted to stroke his face, hold him close and comfort him, to loosen his hair and slide her fingers through the thickness.

"What are you thinking about?" he asked in a quiet voice. He lifted her hand and turned it over to kiss her palm, then closed her fingers as if he wanted her to hold onto his kiss.

"I'm thinking how sad your childhood must have been." *And how I want to hold you.*

"I survived." He moved away, his gaze still on hers. "I'll tell you something I've never told anyone."

"Okay."

"That time when I was ten and the dog bit me?" Graceann nodded.

"A neighbor took me to the ER and stayed with me because my parents were passed out drunk in the house."

She put a hand to her throat. "That's awful."

"It was a long time ago. But I've never been comfortable around dogs after that. Too many bad memories."

"Jake," she whispered. Pity for what he'd gone through mingled with pleasure that he trusted her enough to open his heart. "I'm so sorry."

A door opened and closed somewhere upstairs, making her jump.

"Someone might be coming," Jake said. "Let's make this real."

Before she could respond, he'd tugged her into his arms and his lips were on hers, soft, hot, seductive. Everything faded—the TV, the sounds of the house settling around them, the scents of holly and evergreen. She wound her arms around his neck and melted into him as he deepened the kiss and slipped his tongue into her mouth.

He reclined, bringing her with him until she lay

on top of him. She fit nicely against the hard contours of his body. Her blood felt scorching enough to liquefy her bones. He cradled the back of her head and massaged her scalp as they kissed.

Lost in Jake's passion, his touch, the longing she felt for him, Graceann was barely aware of soft shuffling nearby. The loud sound of a throat clearing finally sliced through her erotic stupor.

Graceann disengaged herself from Jake and twisted her head to look behind her. Lorrie, dressed in pajamas and robe, stood in the doorway, looking contrite. Graceann quickly sat up and straightened her clothes while Jake did the same.

Lorrie grimaced. "I'm sorry. Truly. I came down to get Christian a bottle."

Graceann smoothed a hand over her hair. "You could have used the back stairs to go into the kitchen." She should be grateful Lorrie had interrupted them. Instead, she felt…frustrated.

"I didn't think."

"Dogs and sisters," Jake muttered. "Can't catch a break."

Lorrie frowned. "What?"

"Nothing." Graceann threw Jake a quelling look. "It's time for us to go to bed anyway."

He cocked an eyebrow. "Bed?"

"Alone. We're in my grandmother's house."

Lorrie laughed. "Do what you want. I'll never tell."

Graceann stood. "Goodnight, Jake, Lorrie. See you in the morning."

"Goodnight, sweetheart," Jake said.

Graceann felt him watch her as she walked away. Her insides churned and her legs felt rubbery. Clearly, being alone with Jake Falco was perilous to her self-control.

Chapter Six

YAWNING, JAKE STAGGERED into the kitchen, moving like Frankenstein's monster, which was how he felt every morning until he'd had his first hit of caffeine. After a fitful night with erotic images of Graceann dominating his dreams, he'd given up the fight and gotten out of bed.

The kitchen was deserted at seven o'clock and the house tomb-quiet. Never up this early except when he was on a shoot, he made a beeline for the large single-cup coffee maker perched on the gray granite counter. Heavy white mugs were arranged around the machine. After brewing the strongest cup he could, he took it to the center island and settled onto one of the stools.

Dim sunlight streamed through the opened

blinds, bathing the stainless appliances and gleaming white cabinets. A new day, a clean day to wipe away old memories and start fresh. Guilt and coffee mixed an unsettling brew in him. Maybe he should have been upfront with Graceann from the start and told her his real reason for coming back to Spirit Lake. If he was completely honest with himself, he'd admit some perverse part of him wanted her to accept the man he was now, not her distant memory of a wild guy with a bad rep. Acceptance hadn't come for him in Spirit Lake and he expected it never would. Not with what he had in mind.

Sipping his coffee, his thoughts returned to Graceann, where they had been all night. He wanted her. Had from the first moment he'd spotted her in the diner. No use trying to deny it. He'd wanted her in school too, but she'd been too young, untouchable. But this wasn't high school, and he'd agreed to go along with her charade to get close to her. There were other reasons. Reasons he would keep quiet about for a little longer.

As if he'd conjured her up, Graceann stepped into the room. She froze in the doorway when she saw him. Like a man starved for the sight of his woman, he devoured her with his gaze. Dressed in jeans and a long-sleeved shirt, her dark hair caught in a messy ponytail, her fresh-faced sexuality stirred a yearning in him he'd long ago buried.

He couldn't resist. "Good morning, princess."

Teasing her was too much fun. It also masked his growing feelings for her.

He could swear she growled.

"Not a morning person, I see." He chuckled.

"No." She padded to the coffee maker on feet encased in Indian moccasins and fixed herself a cup, then sat across from him at the counter.

With her hands wrapped around the mug, she took a long sip, then let out a contented sigh as she set the mug down. "The first cup of the day is the best."

"Agreed."

She drank a little more before she fixed him with those sultry bedroom eyes that appeared even larger behind the lenses of her stylish glasses.

"You look good in glasses," he said.

"No, I don't. I always wear my contacts."

"Trust me. You're sexy as hell in those glasses and with that mussed, just-had-sex-hair."

She waved a hand. "Don't go there, Jake. We need to talk. About last night."

"What about it? I was kinda having fun."

"That can't happen again. No more kissing when we're alone."

He grinned. "You liked it."

"That's not the point." She frowned, as if trying to seem severe, but only succeeded in being adorable.

"It's exactly the point." He reached for her hand, but she pulled it out of reach, shaking her head.

Her stubbornness made her even sexier. Damn, he had it bad.

"No more kissing," she repeated in a firm voice. "And why are you up so early?"

"Same reason as you, I suppose."

"*I* couldn't sleep."

"Neither could I." He smiled and leaned closer. "I dreamt of you and what I'd like to do with you."

"I didn't dream about you. And stop with the seductive talk."

"You're a terrible liar." He shot her a wicked grin. "You think I'm seductive?"

She shook her head, clearly not prepared to answer, and drank more coffee. As she sipped, her gaze went to his right forearm, bared by the T-shirt he wore. Frowning, she set down her mug. "Is that a tattoo of a falcon?"

He ran his hand over the tattoo. "I've had it a long time. Got it the week before I graduated high school."

"So you *did* like being called The Falcon."

"Falcons are predators. I got this to remind me that some day I'd crush my enemies."

"That's harsh." She settled back onto her stool, as far away from him as she could manage.

Jake could swear the temperature in the room dropped a few degrees. So Graceann wasn't an eye-for-an-eye sort of woman. No surprises there.

"I felt harsh back then. Don't worry, princess.

I've mellowed since. The falcon now tells me to soar, to follow my own path, that I'm the only one responsible for my life."

"That sounds better." She met his gaze again. "Exactly what path do you follow? What type of work do you do?"

"I need more coffee." He ambled over to the coffee maker and brewed another cup, his back to her. "I've done lots of things in my life. I've been a waiter, a house painter. I write a little." All true.

"What have you written?"

"Nothing you would have heard of." Coffee done, he carried his full mug back to the counter and sat. "Forget about me. Tonight is Christmas Eve. What are the plans? I need to know what I'm facing so I can make a good impression on your family."

She rubbed a tapered index finger along the gray and silver granite. He liked that she wore light pink nail polish on her short nails and not the dragon-lady red so many women in his world favored.

"I have to go into town today," she said, lifting her eyes. "I want to get a few gifts for the family. I want you to go with me. We have to keep up appearances."

He held out his hands. "Hey, I've been doing my part. Engaged couples can't keep their hands to themselves. I'm only doing what's expected, but you seem to have an issue with that."

"You really are impossible."

"But you like it." He grinned over the rim of his mug.

She laughed. "You keep believing that."

He studied her. In the early morning sunlight, she appeared younger, more innocent. Most of the women he'd known in the past had been hardened by life. And many of the women he met in his line of work now were overly aggressive, coarsened by their lifestyles, as if they'd left their softer selves in another life. "Don't ever change, Graceann."

"What does that mean?"

"Always stay sweet."

Her eyes widened in surprise and she swallowed. "Let's get off that subject. It's agreed, we go into town today?"

"Sure. I should probably pick up a few gifts for your family from me."

"You don't have to do that."

"I want to."

She smiled. "That would be nice. Tonight the whole family, except Grandmom and the children, will go to Midnight Mass. You'll be expected to go."

His chest tightened. "I haven't been in a church since my First Communion."

"Your family didn't go to church?"

"Nope. We didn't much celebrate Christmas either."

She reached out and touched his hand where it rested on the counter. "That's too bad. I think church and the holidays are good for kids."

He turned his hand over to grasp hers, holding it tight. He felt a surge of triumph when she didn't try to pull away. "You're probably right, but we weren't like your family."

"I know you have no siblings, but what about other family? Grandparents, cousins, aunts?"

The loneliness he'd learned years ago to keep at bay threatened to break through. He beat it back. "No one." He shook his head. "My dad was from Pittsburgh. He was estranged from his family. I think my mom was originally from down in Delaware. She never talked about her family."

Sadness softened Graceann's eyes. "I can't imagine not being close to my family. I love them all so much."

"I know you do, and they're good people, but maybe you need to separate from them a little."

"What do you mean?" She pulled her hand free.

"You're thirty years old. I don't get this whole subterfuge you're putting on. Tell them the truth. You have a right to live your life the way you want. They can't control you."

"I don't want to hurt them. And you have no right to tell me how to handle my family."

"I don't mean to upset you, but you've got to break the ties sometime. Or at least loosen them."

She opened her mouth to speak when footsteps cut into the tense atmosphere. They turned toward the doorway leading to the back stairs.

Rubbing her eyes, Lorrie, dressed in the same pajamas and robe she'd had on late last night when she'd interrupted them in the great room, sauntered in. "Hey, you two." She headed for the coffee maker. While her coffee brewed, she turned to them. "You're up early." She grinned. "Or maybe you haven't been to sleep yet."

"Lorrie, that's crude," Graceann said.

Jake smiled at Graceann's indignation. Her combination of sexy and naïve shot a dose of desire through him, and he shifted in his seat.

"I'm sorry," Lorrie said. "That *was* crude. Blame it on sleep deprivation. Christian is teething. You'll see what I mean when you have your own kids."

When she turned away to fix her coffee, Jake glanced at Graceann. Her face had flushed a becoming shade of pink.

He saluted her with his mug. Her face got pinker.

Cradling her coffee mug, Lorrie settled onto one of the stools around the counter. She sipped, then set down her cup and said to Graceann, "Did you tell Jake about Steven?"

"I was about to when you came in."

"Steven?" He shifted his gaze from one woman to the other.

Graceann rubbed a hand along the counter top as if lost in thought, then met his eyes. "Steven is an old boyfriend from college. He's moved to this area and

Mom invited him to spend Christmas with us and stay a few days."

Jake managed to keep his expression neutral as a twinge of hurt settled in his chest. He wondered if Graceann's mother had invited the other guy after she'd met Jake because she wasn't happy with her daughter's choice of fiancé. He was only playing a part, he reminded himself. If he and Graceann really were in love, her family would know the whole truth about him. They might approve. Anyway, what her family thought of him wouldn't matter. Only Graceann would matter. Yet, a part of him wanted acceptance from her family, fake fiancé or no.

Graceann gave him an embarrassed smile. "I'm sorry, Jake. Lorrie and I both told Mom she shouldn't have done that, but Mom's stubborn."

"And she has her own agenda," he said. "She evidently likes this other guy."

"I don't care what her agenda is," Graceann said. "You're my fiancé and that's all there is to it." As if she'd realized what she'd said, she clamped her mouth shut.

"Jake, don't worry about our mother," Lorrie said.

"I'm not, but I hope to get her to like me."

"She will," Graceann said. "Daddy seems to like you."

"Maybe," he said with a shrug.

Graceann took a large swig of coffee and set

down the mug, then stood. "I need to get dressed. Meet me downstairs in an hour and we'll head for town?"

"Sure thing, boss," he said. "And wear your glasses today." When she shot him a puzzled look, he smiled and said, "Please."

Graceann shook her head as she walked from the room. The graceful sway of her hips sent blood rushing to his lower regions. He needed more coffee, but with Lorrie there, he had to stay put for a while or risk exposing his burgeoning lust for Graceann.

Jake parked the BMW on Main Street and hopped out. He walked around to the other side to open the door for Graceann, but she'd already exited and waited for him on the sidewalk. He locked the car with the remote key. "Nice car. I ought to get one."

"Do you have a car?" she asked, cocking her head toward him.

"I have a Maserati."

She laughed. "You would."

He laughed with her. He'd learned a long time ago how effective it could be to tell the truth in jest.

"Where to first, princess?"

She pointed down the street. "The wine store is two blocks away. I want to get Daddy his favorite wine. I could have gotten it in New York, but I didn't want to carry it all the way here."

As they walked, Jake scanned the street, lined with upscale boutiques and restaurants, a far cry from the dingy shops he remembered. Spirit Lake had rebuilt itself into a trendy mountain town. The mouth-watering aroma of tomato and basil from the pizza place mingled with the scent of sizzling beef from the Asian restaurant, giving him hunger pangs.

Green and red lights hung across the narrow street, and red foil stars swung on the streetlamps. Even the other shoppers carried a festive air as they went about their business. The town had never looked this clean and happy when he was growing up here.

Bells rung by Salvation Army volunteers on both sides of the street added to the holiday atmosphere. When they passed the Salvation Army kettle, Jake pulled a twenty-dollar bill from his wallet and dropped it into the kettle.

"That's awfully generous," Graceann said.

"Not really. I know what it's like to be on the receiving end of charity."

The softness in her gaze touched his heart. He didn't want her pity. He took her hand in his. "Let's go. Lead the way."

At the shop, she chose her wine and headed to the counter. Jake perused the shelves, selecting a few bottles, and followed her.

She glanced at the wine in his cart. "I've never heard of that brand."

"It's a boutique winery in Napa Valley," he said. "I'm surprised to find it here. A buddy and his wife own the winery. I thought a few bottles would make good gifts for your dad and Andrew."

"You know people who own a winery, but you don't drink? And you know someone who works on movies?"

"I get around."

She frowned but didn't say anything more.

An hour later, they'd bought toys for Isabella and Christian, scarves for Graceann's mom, sister, and grandmother. Strolling to the car, they passed a boutique of high-end women's clothing.

Jake grabbed Graceann's hand. "Let's go in here. I want to buy you a gift."

"You don't have to give me anything."

"I can't have your family think I didn't give you a Christmas gift."

"The engagement ring is my gift."

She looked so serious and so gorgeous as she stood there arguing with him, her dark brown hair spread out over the shoulders of her olive green jacket. The scarf around her neck, in shades of green, changed her eyes to the deep color of holly leaves. She'd worn her glasses, as he'd asked. When she'd come downstairs ready for their shopping trip wearing them, pleasure had stirred in him.

He pulled her into the store. "Don't argue. I'm your fiancé and I'm buying you a gift."

The saleswoman showed them dresses and purses as they wandered through the small, elegant shop. Jake shook his head at each selection. "I want something special for my fiancé."

A mannequin wearing a delicate shawl of pale green silk shot with gold thread caught his eye. "Can we see that wrap?"

The saleswoman hurried to take it off the mannequin, then handed it to Jake. He pulled the soft fabric through his hands, then turned to Graceann. "You said your parents are having a big New Year's Eve party. This shawl matches your eyes. Maybe you can wear it to the party."

Graceann's eyes lit up as she fingered the gauzy wrap.

"Try it on," the saleswoman said.

Jake laid it over Graceann's shoulders. The green did indeed bring out her eyes.

"It's gorgeous," Graceann said, running a hand over the fabric.

"It's yours." Jake turned to the beaming saleswoman. "We'll take it. Can you gift wrap it?"

With a nod, the woman hurried away, the shawl in her arms.

"Thank you, Jake," Graceann said.

Her smile sent his heart into a tailspin. She parted her full pink lips, inviting his kiss. He bent and brushed his lips over hers. "You're welcome, sweetheart."

"I need a gift for you," she said.

"I don't want anything."

"But you won't have anything to unwrap tomorrow morning."

"That's nothing new. I'll tell your family you've given me the greatest gift of all—you've agreed to be my wife."

"That's corny."

He touched the tip of her nose. "Your family will love it."

Later, juggling packages, they exited the shop. Jake stopped at the door of a doggie boutique. "Maybe we should get a gift for Fluffy. A muzzle would be perfect."

Graceann laughed. "The little yapper would find a way to tear it off." When they passed a stationary store, Graceann stopped. "I know what to get you for Christmas."

"I don't want anything from you."

She handed him her packages. "I'm getting you something anyway. You stay here. I'll be right out."

Fifteen minutes later, carrying a small, wrapped package and smiling like the cat that swallowed the proverbial canary or two, she came out of the shop. "I'm ready."

She took a few of the packages from him before they continued their walk. Jake couldn't remember the last time he'd felt this happy, this carefree.

Graceann did that for him. He never wanted the day to end.

A familiar looking figure hurrying along the opposite sidewalk made Jake stop and stare.

"What is it?" Graceann asked.

He squinted. "Is that Ryan Nelson? What happened to him? He looks like hell." The scrawny man coughed as he held the collar of his coat close and turned a corner out of sight. Jake met Graceann's gaze. "His father was mayor when we were in school. Didn't Nelson go to Princeton?"

She shook her head. "He lost his scholarship when he got arrested for dealing drugs. He's been to rehab many times, but he can't seem to stop using."

Jake released a breath, feeling a smidgen of his old bitterness float away. He'd not been part of Nelson's rich, fast crowd in school, but he'd known about the guy's run-ins with the law, problems his influential father had smoothed away. Jake and his friends had gotten blamed for some of the stunts Nelson and his crowd had pulled. The town was only too eager to believe the worst of the guys from the bad side of town. Looked like Nelson's shenanigans had finally caught up with him. Jake had expected to feel a flash of triumph, but he felt only pity.

"Jake? Are you okay?" Graceann tugged on his arm.

He smiled down at her. "I'm fine. Better than I've been for awhile."

They'd walked a little ways when it was Graceann's turn to freeze and halt in mid-stride.

"What is it?" he asked.

"Steven," she whispered. "Shoot."

A dark-haired guy of average height, his hair cut military short, and wearing an expensive-looking camel overcoat, hurried over to them.

"Graceann," he said when he reached them. "Sweetheart."

He bent as if to kiss her, but she stepped back to press closer to Jake. "Hello, Steven."

His light gray eyes roved over her, insolent and possessive. Jake wanted to grab the guy by the throat.

"Your mother invited me for Christmas," the guy said.

"I know." Graceann turned to Jake. "Steven Craig. Jake Falco. My fiancé."

"I heard you'd gotten engaged." Steven dismissed Jake with cold eyes.

Jake smirked. "Always good to meet *old* friends of my fiancée's."

Steven's features tightened. "When's the wedding?"

"Six months," Graceann said.

"Three months," Jake said at the same time.

Jake and Graceann stared at each other.

"Sorry, darling," Jake said. "I know you need six months to plan, but I can't wait that long."

She stood on tiptoe and kissed him lightly on the lips, then turned to Steven.

"We need to go," she said. "See you tomorrow."

Steven scowled, and Jake laughed as he and Graceann strolled away.

"Nice guy," Jake said.

When they reached the car he unlocked it with the remote key. They stuffed the packages in the trunk and he opened the passenger door for Graceann, then slid into the driver's seat. As they drove away, he said, "How did someone as classy and sweet as you get mixed up with a jerk like that?" He sounded like a real fiancé, a jealous one. He really was beginning to live the part.

"Steven's not so bad when you get to know him. We dated off-and-on for a few years. He didn't want to be exclusive, and that was okay with me. Not many guys asked me out, but Steven always had a string of girlfriends. When he was between girlfriends, he'd date me."

"You put up with that? And what was wrong with the guys you went to college with? If you were mine, I'd never let you go." Damn! He couldn't believe he'd said that. He had to stop this!

"Oh," she said, clearly startled.

He didn't have to see her to know she'd blushed.

"I don't know why I put up with him," she said

slowly, recovering from her moment of surprise. "Maybe I didn't care enough."

"Baby, whatever the reason, you've got to learn to stand up for yourself."

"I've learned. Since I've been in New York I've become independent and I can take up for myself. I couldn't run my business if I didn't know how to negotiate with my suppliers and customers. I wouldn't put up with a guy like Steven now."

"But you're afraid to tell your family to let you live your life on your terms."

She sighed. "I know, but I'm working on that. Jake, please don't tell me what to do."

He hated the bitterness that rose in him. "Forget it."

Tension rode in the car with them all the way back to the house. Jake had enjoyed being alone with Graceann, enjoyed spending time with her in town. Until he and his big mouth had ruined the day. He needed to remember his place in her life.

He was just the temporary help.

Chapter Seven

IT HAD STARTED TO SNOW while they were at church. Graceann couldn't remember the last time she'd felt so peaceful. Giving a contented sigh, she stared out the windshield at the gently falling flakes as Jake maneuvered the BMW through the narrow streets on their way back to the house. Lorrie, Andrew and Graceann's parents rode in front of them in Lorrie's minivan.

"It's so beautiful with the Christmas lights reflecting on the pure white snow," Graceann said. "It's a silent, magical picture."

Jake chuckled. "Feeling poetic, are you?"

She laughed. "A little. I get carried away during the holidays. We couldn't ask for a more beautiful Christmas Eve. Or rather Christmas morning." She reached over to increase the volume on the car's radio. "Listen. It's Bing Crosby singing *White Christmas*." She clapped her hands. "No one does that song better than he does."

"You really love Christmas."

"It's my favorite holiday. Isn't it yours?"

"It never was." His voice thickened. "Until now."

Graceann stared at his strong profile with his hawk-like nose and proud chin. His words and the huskiness of his voice sent her temperature soaring and she loosened her scarf. She wanted to tell him he could drop the act because they were alone. But he'd sounded so sincere. And for a little while she wanted to believe the fantasy that she and Jake really were a couple in love.

"It's been awhile since I've seen snow," he said, his attention on the road that was swiftly becoming slippery. "I've almost forgotten how to drive in the stuff."

"It's not cold where you live?"

"I try to follow the sun."

Enigmatic as always, she thought, as she snuggled down into the soft leather seat. She would allow nothing to mar the peace and contentment she felt at the moment. "Church was nice, wasn't it?"

"I enjoyed the service, to my surprise. The choir was great."

He reached across the car's console and took her hand in his. His touch warmed her through her wool gloves, and with another contented sigh, she scrunched farther down in her seat and looked out the side window, watching the soft snowflakes float around them. Jake had seemed enthralled at church, interested in everything around him. The clothes he'd chosen to wear reflected the importance he'd attached to this night, which pleased her. He wore his black leather jacket, but he'd dressed in black slacks and a white shirt instead of his usual jeans and sweater. And rather than boots, he wore black shoes that looked like fine Italian leather. Others in the church had shot curious stares his way, and she wondered if any of them recognized him as the infamous Falcon. Thankfully, unlike most times, her parents didn't stay to talk to the other parishioners. With the lateness of the hour, her parents had merely waved and exchanged Christmas greetings with their friends.

She'd been proud to be seen with Jake. Truth be told, she felt good whenever she was with him no matter how he dressed. That thought came out of nowhere and sent her head spinning. What, if anything, was going on between them?

Determined to tuck away her uncomfortable thoughts, she slid him a glance. She'd dwell on things later. "Aren't you cold in that leather jacket?"

"A little, but I'm a big boy. I can handle it."

"Those nice shoes you're wearing will get ruined in this weather."

"Don't worry about it. They're only shoes."

He seemed to take everything in stride and didn't obsess over his appearance like some men she knew. But then most men didn't have the innate confidence of Jake Falco.

Graceann glanced at the car's digital clock as they pulled into Grandmom's driveway. Two o'clock. She yawned.

"Tired?" Jake released her hand and turned off the ignition.

"I am. Isabella will have all of us up in a few hours. She's three now so Santa's real to her. She doesn't understand about letting grownups sleep."

He laughed. "I don't need a lot of sleep. But let's get you to bed."

When they got inside the quiet house, everyone said their goodnights in hushed tones. The others trooped softly upstairs, but Jake held back. Graceann, with a foot on the bottom step, gave him a questioning look.

"I'll stay down here for awhile. I'm not sleepy." He grinned. "But I am hungry. I thought I might have some of that delicious fried chicken your grandmother made for dinner tonight."

"Okay. See you in a few hours."

A half hour later Graceann lay in bed, wide-awake. She hadn't heard Jake come upstairs. She needed to sleep, but wanted to be with him even more. Refusing to examine why, she slid out of bed and slipped a thick robe over her short nightgown.

She pulled the robe's sash tight and jammed her feet into slippers, then padded down the back stairs to the kitchen where a dim light glowed. Jake sat at the center counter, a plate of cold chicken in front of him. A large glass of water was set next to the plate. He'd taken off his jacket and rolled up the sleeves of his shirt, exposing muscled arms with a sprinkling of fine dark hairs. The light caught his falcon tattoo, seeming to make its wings flutter. Christmas carols, the volume low, played on the radio.

He'd loosened his hair, and the thick midnight black strands flowed to his shoulders. Her throat went dry and her heart thumped, drowning out the sounds of the music.

He looked up. His blue eyes lit with awareness, sharpening her own awareness of him. Hot-cold shivers slid down her arms.

"What are you doing up?" he asked, his voice soft and husky.

"I couldn't sleep." She moved into the room and went to the cabinet to get a glass, then filled the glass with water and sat across from him. "This is nice." She scanned the dimly-lit kitchen. "Serene. The Christmas music is the perfect touch."

"I never enjoyed Christmas carols before. I thought they were corny. But I don't feel that way now. They go with the peacefulness here. You're lucky to have such a loving family."

"I know." She locked gazes with him. "Jake, even though we started out with a business arrangement, I'm glad you're here. And I'm glad we could give you a good Christmas. I hope it's one you'll always remember."

"I'll always remember it. And you." His voice softened and he looked away. She wondered if he could be uncomfortable. The Falcon, uncomfortable? That was a new one.

When he turned back to her, his full lips tilted in a teasing grin. He was again the cocky, confident guy she'd come to know. "We both seem to have trouble sleeping lately."

"It's the holidays. Lots going on." She wrapped her hands around the glass but didn't drink.

"Baby, it's a lot more than the holidays keeping us awake. I have a cure for what ails us—Falco's never-fail insomnia remedy."

"I'm sure you have many satisfied customers," she said primly, but she couldn't stop the smile that broke free. She took a long swig of water, moistening her dust-dry throat. Too bad the liquid couldn't extinguish the desire crackling in her like a yuletide fire.

"I think you'd enjoy what I have in mind."

Her gaze swept him. *Oh, yes. I know I would.* "Let's not go there," she said instead. She might not be as experienced as Jake, but she wasn't inexperienced, as he seemed to think. While it wasn't her usual style, a certain amount of primness seemed to be the only thing keeping her safe these days. Somehow during their short time together, she needed to refrain from proving herself otherwise. But could she manage?

His grin widened, and he pushed the plate of chicken toward her. "Have something to eat."

She shook her head. "Not hungry."

"Your grandmother makes some mean chicken." He took another leg from the plate and bit into it, then wiped his mouth with his napkin.

"Grandmom's a good cook."

Finished with the leg, he wiped his mouth again and set the plate aside. "What about you? Can you cook?"

"When I have to."

"You'd be surprised at the women I know who couldn't boil water if their lives depended on it."

She raised an eyebrow. "What kind of women do you know?"

He laughed. "I don't kiss and tell, Ms. Palmer."

Heat spread over her chest, up her neck, to her face. Of course, he wasn't the kind of guy who boasted about his conquests. Avoiding eye contact, she ran her fingers over the rivulets of water on her glass.

"Not wearing your engagement ring?" he asked.

She raised her gaze to his. "I don't wear jewelry to bed."

He grinned. "What else don't you wear to bed?"

"Stop it, Jake."

He held his hands up in surrender. "I promise to be good, or at least to behave. You won't let me be as good as I can be."

The teasing note in his voice told her he wouldn't try very hard to behave, and that thought sent a hot curl of excitement through her. She wanted him to misbehave. There was no use denying it. Getting to know him, the real Jake Falco, was more exciting than her memories of him. She wanted him.

"The ring you designed is beautiful," he said, breaking into her thoughts. "You're very talented."

With effort, she pushed aside her lustful ramblings, at least for the moment. "Thanks." Finished with her water, she slid the empty glass away.

"How did you start designing jewelry?"

"I've always been artistic. Get that from my mother's mother. I taught myself to work with gems and metals. I earned extra spending money at college making and selling jewelry. Knowing what I wanted to do, I took some business courses in school and made a strategic plan. When I graduated, I took the money Grandmom and my parents gave me for a graduation gift, got an efficiency apartment in the East Village, joined an artistic co-op where I could sell my jewelry, and here I am."

"You're one smart lady." He studied her. "Business must be good if you can afford to pay me." He grinned. "And to think I cut my fee for you."

She couldn't help smiling. "My business is growing. At first, my parents gave me a monthly stipend, but now I support myself." She shrugged. "I'm not exactly living the high life, but I'm saving money, building a reputation and gaining more customers all the time." Leaning closer, she said, "And I can afford to pay you."

He sipped his water and watched her over the rim of the glass, then set down the glass. "You should be proud of your success. Your family should be proud of you."

"I am and they are."

"Good," he said with a smile.

They stared at each other. Yearning pulsed deep inside in her, making her suck in a breath.

Until she recognized the song playing on the radio, *Grandma Got Run Over by a Reindeer*. Nerves and the comical lyrics made Graceann shake her head and laugh. Jake joined her.

When the song ended, she pushed up from the stool. "On that note, I guess I'd better go back to bed."

"Me, too. Let me get rid of this empty plate." Jake scraped the leftover chicken bits into the garbage compacter and rinsed the plate before putting it into the dishwasher, then he turned to Graceann. "After you."

He followed her up the stairs, so close she inhaled his woodsy masculine scent. With him so close and she clad only in her nightclothes, excitement began to mount in her.

When they reached her room, she pushed the door open and turned to him. The dim hall light reflected in his eyes, eyes that held desire and something that made her breath hitch.

"I'll see you later." She took a step back into the room.

"I'd better come in with you, in case there's a bogeyman hiding under your bed." He followed her and quietly closed the door.

Then he pulled her into his arms. Up close and personal. She leaned into him, seeking his heat, and splayed her hands on his chest. The steady beat of his heart vibrated through her. "I think the only thing I need to fear is the man standing before me."

"Are you afraid of me?"

"I'm afraid of what you make me feel."

"How do I make you feel?"

She licked her lips. "Like I want and need something that's just out of reach."

"It's not out of reach, Graceann." He took her lips in a crushing kiss that shattered any control she still had. She opened her mouth, giving him entry, kissing him with a wild abandon she'd never felt before. With a low, guttural groan, she wound her arms around his neck and pressed close, melding her body to his strong frame. She tunneled unsteady hands through his hair. It was as silky and thick as it looked.

He kissed the corners of her mouth and the curve of her throat. Needy cries erupted from deep inside her. As he kissed his way to her chest, his fingers fumbled with the sash on her robe. It fell open and he slid his hands inside and up her ribcage to cup her breasts. Her nipples puckered and her breasts strained against the thin satin of her nightgown. He caressed her breasts, pushing them together, then kissed the hollow between them.

Graceann threw back her head, willingly giving him whatever he wanted. He backed her up against the wall. His hands spanned her waist and he feasted on one breast and then the other through the soft material.

Fisting her hands through his hair, she drew him closer. His erection pressed against her stomach. When he cupped her buttocks and lifted her, she wrapped her legs around his waist. Her body on fire, she cried out. His kiss swallowed her moans.

He ended the kiss and rested his forehead on hers, his breathing harsh. "You're amazing. What am I going to do about you?"

She slid down him and pulled away. "Make love to me, Jake. I need you."

A door slammed somewhere in the house. She tried to ignore it. All that mattered now was her and Jake and her fierce desire for him.

He released a tortured breath. "I want you, Graceann. So much. But I won't take advantage of you."

She cupped his face between her hands. "You're not taking advantage."

"You've lived a sheltered life. You always have. I'm not the kind of guy you're used to. Hell, I'm not the kind of guy you deserve."

"Don't sell yourself short, Jake. You're exactly what I need."

He brushed a whisper-soft kiss on her lips. "It's been a long day and you're tired. After a few hours of sleep you'll feel differently. Goodnight, princess."

With that, he slipped out the door.

Graceann sank onto her bed. Who would have thought? The Falcon was a gentleman. Of all times to show his chivalrous side, he had to pick tonight. She sighed and touched her breasts. They were tight and hot, pushing against the confining nightgown.

For sure, she wouldn't sleep, not now.

Chapter Eight

A CHILD'S LOUD SQUEAL jolted Graceann awake. Groaning, she burrowed deeper into her covers. Isabella was up and sounded determined to go downstairs to see what Santa brought her.

Graceann opened her eyes slowly. Her eyelids felt like sandpaper. She rolled over and glanced at the small nightstand clock. Barely seven! With another groan, she put her pillow over her head. She'd gotten to sleep less than three hours ago. A high-pitched shriek along with the sounds of footsteps and hushed voices in the hallway told her she'd get no more sleep this morning. Besides, she wanted to watch Isabella open her gifts.

She threw aside the covers, slid out of bed and sat on the edge with her feet on the floor, blinking to adjust to the weak sunlight sneaking through the blinds. Her eyes watered. If just the slight bit of sunlight bothered her, she was in for a hell of a day.

There was another reason the day might be a tad awkward. The memory of Jake and his kisses and caresses early this morning cut through the cobwebs in her brain. Those kisses! His lips and hands touching her, fondling her breasts. What had gotten into her? What about preserving Jake's image of her? What had happened to her common sense, to their "business" arrangement?

She'd had a sexual relationship with Michael, and had enjoyed it. But whatever desire she'd felt for him was a pale imitation of the real passion, of the wildness, Jake incited in her.

Edgy and agitated, she jumped out of bed and headed to her attached bathroom. She needed to splash cold water on her face. A little while later, dressed in jeans, a sweater, and her favorite moccasins, she opened her bedroom door. And came face-to-face with Jake.

"Merry Christmas, princess. I was about to knock."

"Merry Christmas to you, too," she said, her voice low and breathy.

He scanned her face, stopping at her mouth, then his gaze dropped lower before meeting her eyes again. "Did you sleep at all?" His voice was gravelly, as if he hadn't slept either.

"A little. What about you?"

He brushed his thumb over her cheekbone. "Not much. I couldn't stop thinking about you."

Her whole body was instantly on fire. She wanted to pull him into her room and make wild love, but that was her libido talking. She needed to get a grip. Laughter and Isabella's excited cries provided Graceann a much-needed distraction.

"We'd better go down," she said.

Jake stepped back. "Yeah."

They found the family in the great room gathered around the tree. Grandmom, a mug of coffee in hand, sat on one of the loveseats. The others relaxed on the sofa and watched Isabella pull gifts from underneath the tree. Baby Christian slept in Lorrie's arms, oblivious to the tumult.

As Jake and Graceann headed to a small table set with coffee and bagels, Fluffy came running into the room, yapping at Jake.

"Fluffy, stop it," Grandmom said. "Come over here."

With one last bark, the dog trotted over to Grandmom and sat at her feet.

Jake's features relaxed and he let out an audible sigh. After Graceann and Jake each poured a cup of coffee and slathered bagels with cream cheese, they settled onto the other loveseat.

When Isabella lifted a new baby doll from a box, she squealed, then holding the doll, she ran over to Jake and waved it.

Laughing, he set his mug on the coffee table and picked up the little girl, settling her on his lap. "What a nice doll," he said. "Will you let me play with it some time?"

With a solemn expression, Isabella shook her head and clutched her doll tighter. When she began to squirm, Jake set her down, and she ran back to the tree and more gifts.

As Isabella, then the others, opened their gifts, Graceann slid a glance at Jake. She'd never seen him smile so much. His smile lit up his face and eyes, making him look younger and vulnerable. A little bit more of her heart melted.

The women liked the scarves she and Jake gave them. The wine Jake gave to her father and brother-in-law was a big hit, too.

"I know the owners of that winery," Jake said.

Andrew's eyebrows rose. "Sweet!"

The whole family seemed to have accepted Jake. Except her mom, who gave Jake tight-lipped looks that made Graceann's chest clench with annoyance. Graceann was giving her mother what she wanted and she still wasn't happy. Reminding herself her engagement to Jake was a farce, Graceann took calming breaths. The fake engagement had started to feel like the real deal.

"Open your gift from Jake," Lorrie urged.

Graceann got up from the loveseat and grabbed the gold foil-wrapped package with the green silk shawl from under the tree. She opened it slowly, drawing out the suspense for the others, then held it up for the rest to see, pretending to be surprised.

"It's beautiful," Lorrie said. "It's so you. Try it on."

"It's lovely," Grandmom said with a smile for Jake. "Jake has wonderful taste."

"Let me put it on you." Jake stood, took the wrap from Graceann and draped it over her shoulders, lifting her hair off her neck. He brushed his hands up her arms as he bent to softly kiss her nape.

Jake was certainly playing his part. Her skin tingled where he touched, and his hot breath on the back of her neck sent delicious shivers along her spine. "Thank you for the gift," she said softly.

The others, except for Graceann's mother, watched, grinning. A hot flush spread over Graceann's face.

"Open your gift, Jake," she said quickly. She picked up a package wrapped in silver with a red bow and handed it to him.

When he'd unwrapped it and pulled out the leather-bound journal she'd given him, he looked at her with amazement, then gave her a wide smile. "Thank you."

"You said you like to write. I'm hoping now you'll find the incentive."

"I will." He kissed her long and hard.

Her breathing ragged, she finally pulled away. She could feel her mother's steady gaze. Graceann's face burned hotter and she knew she must be as red as the brightest Christmas bulb. She needed to tell Jake to tone it down. Like he'd listen.

When they'd finished opening the gifts and eaten more bagels, Graceann and Jake went upstairs to shower and dress. At the door to her room, Jake cupped her shoulders and turned her toward him. He leaned down and gave her a slow, sweet kiss, running his tongue over the seam of her lips until she opened to him.

After long, lust-filled minutes, they separated. Graceann gazed into his eyes. "What are you doing, Jake?"

"I'm kissing you. What does it feel like?"

"I've told you we don't have to put on an act when we're alone. I'm beginning to think you're enjoying this way too much."

He skimmed fingers over her lips. "I am enjoying it. A lot. And, baby, it stopped being an act a long time ago."

"You didn't want me earlier today. You walked away."

"I'm not good for you, but that doesn't stop me from wanting you."

Frowning, she stepped back, fighting the adrenaline rush of excitement his words provoked. "I need to get changed." She slipped into her room and shut the door, wishing she could lock out her growing hunger for him as easily.

Graceann took extra time with her appearance, telling herself she wanted to look especially nice for Christmas. "Who are you kidding?" she asked her reflection before heading downstairs. "You're doing this to excite Jake."

Her bad girl self was coming out to play. She'd dressed in a black wool pencil skirt and green silk blouse and she put on a pair of earrings that looked like miniature green Christmas balls. Kate had given them to her last year. Walking carefully on her black suede stilettos, she held the handrail as she made her way down the stairs to the living room. What would Jake say if he knew she was wearing a red thong?

The men were already there, drinks in hand, snacking on appetizers. She could use a drink herself. They wouldn't have lunch today because they'd have an early, big dinner. As she entered the room, her attention focused solely on Jake, listening intently to something Andrew was saying.

Jake looked delicious as always. Today he wore a tan shirt, unbuttoned at the throat to expose a scattering of fine dark hairs, and black slacks. His hair was neatly tied back with a leather cord in his usual ponytail.

He turned. The pure masculine appreciation in his sapphire eyes stole her breath. Everything else faded as they stared at each other.

She smiled. Mission accomplished.

"Graceann," her dad said, distracting her from Jake and her lustful thoughts. "Come in and have a glass of this Pinot Grigio Jake gave me. It's some of the best I've tasted."

She walked into the room on legs that wobbled like jelly. Looking at Jake had her hormones revved up like a train speeding toward derailment. It seemed her plan to excite him had managed to get both of them worked up—and they still had an entire evening to get through.

She took the proffered glass of white wine from her father and sat on the loveseat next to Jake. "Where are the kids?" she asked Andrew.

"Both sleeping, thank God. Isabella wore herself out."

Jake laughed. "That's what Christmas is all about, the kids."

Graceann sipped the wine. Her father was right. The wine was wonderful. Strange that Jake, who didn't drink alcohol, would know the owner of a winery that made such a premium wine like this. She took another sip and slanted a glance at Jake. He smiled. She gathered he hadn't had a childhood filled with fond memories, yet he seemed relaxed and happy here with her family. Feeling more relaxed herself, she settled into her seat.

"Where are the others?" she asked.

"Your grandmother's napping," her father

said. "Your mother and Lorrie are in the kitchen. They say they need to start dinner, but I suspect they're drinking wine and trying to escape from the rest of us."

The shrill ring of the doorbell disturbed the calm. Graceann looked at the clock over the mantle. Twelve. She groaned inwardly. Steven was here.

Graceann started to get up, but Lorrie came from the kitchen at the back of the house and hurried to the door, her heels clicking on the marble floor of the foyer. Their mother was close behind her.

Graceann heard the door open, then Lorrie saying, "Merry Christmas, Steven. Nice to see you again."

"Steven! Merry Christmas," her mother said, more animated than Graceann had heard her in the past few days.

Suppressing the urge to roll her eyes, Graceann looked at Jake. His mouth had set into a thin line. Then Steven, holding several wrapped packages, and followed by the two women, stepped into the room. "Merry Christmas, everyone." Dressed in a black overcoat brushed with snow, he looked around the room, arrogance and confidence in every line of his body.

He set his packages on a nearby table and walked over to Graceann. Bending, he placed a kiss on her cheek.

"Merry Christmas, Graceann. You look fantastic."

She hadn't dressed for him. She'd dressed for Jake. She had the uncomfortable feeling Steven was the Grinch, come to steal her Christmas spirit.

Ignoring Jake, Steven greeted the others. He slipped off his overcoat and handed it to Lorrie. Dressed in a dark blue suit Graceann suspected cost a few thousand dollars, a snowy white shirt, the cuffs sporting gold cufflinks, and a blue striped tie that perfectly complemented his suit, he was the picture of a successful lawyer.

Graceann slid closer to Jake. She preferred Jake's natural sexiness to Steven's polished fashion-magazine look.

"Steven, you remember Jake," she said.

Forced to openly acknowledge Jake, Steven looked over. "How's it going, Falco?"

"Couldn't be better." Jake put his arm around Graceann's shoulders.

After a half hour of awkward conversation, the women excused themselves to go into the kitchen to prepare dinner. Eager to escape Steven's possessive stares, Graceann didn't complain about the women doing all the cooking.

Her mom had put the turkey in the oven earlier and had prepared the green bean casserole the day before. Lorrie made her signature dish of scalloped potatoes while Graceann set about making the cranberry stuffing, which they cooked separately from the turkey. Christmas songs played on the radio, bathing the room in cheerfulness. The holiday spirit didn't reach Graceann, however. She seethed over her mother's meddling. Steven's presence had put a damper on her Christmas joy.

"Need any help?" Jake poked his head into the kitchen.

"Can you make mac and cheese?" Lorrie asked. "Isabella loves it and she won't eat any of what we're cooking."

He grinned. "I make a mean mac and cheese. Point me to the ingredients."

As if someone flipped on a bright Christmas light, Graceann's melancholy mood lifted. Smiling at Jake, she set about putting the ingredients out for him.

Working side-by-side with Jake, the Christmas music held new meaning. Contentment settled over her, and her body seemed to melt with his nearness. As if he could read her thoughts, he looked over and gave her an intimate smile.

Graceann noticed her mom stealing looks at Jake. Why couldn't her mother see what a great guy he was?

Damn, she was thinking like a woman in love.

No, that couldn't be.

She smoothed a hand down her body-hugging skirt. She wasn't in love with Jake. In lust maybe, but not love. The Christmas music, the scents of cinnamon and pine, the bright decorations, had all put her in a romantic bubble that would burst like an icy water balloon once the holidays were over. What was she *thinking*, wanting to seduce Jake into sleeping with her?

"How's it going in here?" Steven, glass of wine in hand, strolled into the room.

Graceann bristled. "We're good. Everything's under control."

Beside her, she felt Jake stiffen.

"Kitchen duty, Falco?" Steven asked with a jeer.

"Best place in the house, surrounded by beautiful women," Jake said.

Lorrie snickered. Graceann smiled. Her mother, a confused look on her face, stared at the two men. Her mom should have expected this, having inviting Steven when Jake was there.

The men faced off like two bucks, antlers ready, preparing to fight to the death. *Have a Holly, Jolly Christmas* played on the radio. Graceann wanted to put her head in her hands and groan. Her mother might have started the ball rolling, but she herself had given it a huge push downhill, dressing to entice Jake.

Clearly, Steven thought she'd done it for him.

A holly, jolly Christmas indeed.

Chapter Nine

GRACEANN WAS DETERMINED to enjoy their Christmas dinner and not let Steven's presence interfere. He sat across from her, and much as she tried to ignore him, she felt his hot stares. Jake and he paid no attention to each other. If the others at the table noticed, they didn't show it and kept up a lively conversation in between bites of mouth-watering food and sips of luscious wine. When Jake took her hand in his under the table, Graceann threw him a grateful smile and began to relax. Jake understood how Steven's being there upset her.

Afterward, Jake cajoled the men into cleaning up while the women rested. Now, seated on the sofa in the great room, Graceann slipped off her heels, put her feet up on the coffee table and sipped coffee.

Grandmom, a glass of red wine in hand, sat on one of the loveseats. Lorrie relaxed next to Graceann, and their mother sat in a plush chair near the fireplace. Isabella and Christian were once again asleep upstairs.

Christmas music played softly in the background, an accompaniment to the sharp crackle of the fire in the fieldstone hearth fireplace. The scents of bayberry and cinnamon from candles set strategically throughout the room wafted over them. Graceann sighed. She felt full, satisfied…happy.

Her grandmother glanced toward the kitchen where the men worked, then nodded at Graceann. "That Jake of yours is a good man."

Lorrie chuckled. "Anyone who can get Daddy and Andrew to clean the kitchen is a keeper."

Graceann smiled. "None of them seemed to mind, except Steven." She shook her head, wondering if Steven had recently gotten so arrogant, or if he'd always been that way and she hadn't noticed.

Her mother snorted. "Steven is our guest. He should be in here with his coffee, not stuck in the kitchen. I'm sure he didn't expect to work for his meal."

"For God's sake, Mom, get over it," Lorrie said.

"Jake's a guest, too," Graceann said. "He doesn't mind cleaning up."

Her mom put up a hand. "I stand corrected, although we are providing room and board."

Before Graceann could respond, her mother met her gaze, adding, "Jake seems devoted to you, and I want you to be happy. But I pictured you with a man who's more...who's in a more professional line of work."

Jake, devoted to her? She barely heard the rest of her mother's speech. Jake was a hell of an actor if he'd convinced her mother he loved Graceann. He'd told Graceann he wanted her, and she knew his desire was no act. The realization both thrilled and scared her. But love and lust weren't the same, and this felt like more than lust.

Her mother was staring at her, expecting an answer.

Graceann blinked. "Professional? What does that have to do with whether a man will make a good husband?"

"Graceann's right," her grandmother said.

"I agree," Lorrie said with a nod.

A contrite look swept over her mother's face. "I only want you to be happy, Graceann."

"I know, Mom."

Grandmom set her wine glass on the table and rubbed her upper arms.

"Are you cold?" Graceann asked her.

"A little."

"Where's your sweater?"

"On my bed."

Graceann pushed up from the sofa. "I'll get it for you."

She trotted up the stairs and went into Grandmom's room, the largest bedroom in the sprawling house. She found the sweater on the bed and grabbed it, then left and closed the door behind her. As she walked down the hall, she heard footsteps on the stairs and Steven came into view.

He hurried toward her. "Good. You're alone." He gripped her shoulders and backed her against the wall, standing close, too close. His wine-laced breath fanned her cheeks as she held the sweater against her chest like a barrier. She tried to squirm free but he refused to let her go.

"What do you want, Steven? I need to get this sweater to my grandmother."

"Graceann, I know things didn't work out between us, but I'd like to give us another chance. Of all the women I've dated, you're still the one I want to spend the rest of my life with. You'd be a great asset to my career and a great mother to my children. Why do you think I moved here? I figured you'd want to live close to your family once we were married."

"Married? You're delusional, Steven. I'm engaged to someone else. You asked me to marry you once and I said no. I thought we parted as friends."

"Friends?" Steven's gray eyes bored into hers. "That guy you're engaged to isn't our kind, Graceann. He's rough, crude. A woman like you needs someone like me, a man with polish who appreciates money and all it can buy, a man who can give you a comfortable life."

She put a hand on his chest and felt his muscles tense. "None of this is your business. Don't ruin our friendship with all this possessiveness, Steven. Now let go of me. I need to get back downstairs."

"Damn it, Graceann—"

"You heard the lady. Get your hands off her."

Graceann gasped. She hadn't heard Jake come upstairs. She peered around Steven. Jake stood nearby, his body tense, poised for a fight. The look on his face was one of controlled fury.

Muttering another curse, Steven released her and slithered back a few steps. Hands out, palms extended, he faced Jake. "Hey, man, I didn't mean anything by it. The lady and I had a thing going once. She's looking so hot tonight. Can't blame me for trying."

"Get the hell away from my fiancée before I forget I'm in her grandmother's house," Jake snarled.

With a black look at Graceann, as if this were all *her* fault, Steven skirted past Jake and down the stairs.

"Are you okay?" Jake asked, turning to her.

"I'm fine. He doesn't scare me." She clutched her grandmother's sweater tighter against her chest and shook her head. "Was he always a jerk and I never noticed until now?"

Jake stepped closer and brushed strands of hair back from her face. "I think he was always a jerk but you were too sweet to notice."

The intensity in his eyes made her breathing go shallow. "I'm not that sweet, Jake."

"I think you're very sweet." His voice softened. "And delicious."

Her breathing stopped.

He smiled and moved back. "Let's go for a walk to the dock. I think we both need a break. Time to put things back in perspective. Bundle up. I don't want you to be cold."

I could never be cold around you. If anything, I'm overheated. The words pushed into her mind and made her blush. "A walk sounds great. After I bring Grandmom's sweater to her."

Fifteen minutes later, wearing her knee-high boots and bundled into a long coat, scarf and gloves, Graceann strolled beside Jake over the wooden walkway to the dock. He wore his black leather jacket, but had borrowed gloves and a brightly colored striped scarf from Andrew.

"The scarf suits you," she said.

Grinning, he looked down at her. "Really? I don't see myself as a striped scarf kind of guy."

She laughed and grabbed his hand. It felt right to hold onto him.

"Your brother-in-law strikes me as an uptight sort," Jake said. "What's he doing with a scarf like this?"

"Lorrie gave it to him. Andrew is the button-down type. Even though he's a great guy, I think Lorrie would like him to be a little more exciting."

They'd reached the dock and, still holding hands, stood near the edge and looked over the water. Broken bits of ice floated in the inky blackness. The snow had stopped and clouds smudged the sky, letting the moon peek through. She inhaled the clean, crisp, pine-laced air.

Jake squeezed her hand. "What kind of guy do you want, Ms. Palmer? A buttoned-down insurance type like Andrew or someone with a little danger?"

Staring out over the water, she formulated her answer before she turned to look up at him. "I want a decent guy who doesn't lie to me, who treats me with respect, and who won't cheat. And who totally loves me."

"That's a tall order," he said quietly. "Most guys I know couldn't live up to that."

"I won't settle for anything less."

"And you shouldn't. You deserve the best." His gaze locked with hers. "You don't want a guy who lies, yet you're not being truthful with your family about me." His voice had softened.

"I know it's hypocritical. Believe me, I feel guilty." She blew out a breath and watched as it frosted in the air. "I'm in too deep with this whole scheme and I don't know how to get out of it."

"Easy. Tell them the truth."

"Do you always tell the truth?" she asked, meeting his gaze again.

His mouth set in a tight line and he glanced out over the water. "Not always."

There he was, being secretive again. Jake had more layers than Grandmom's six-layer coconut cake. Graceann suspected that, unlike her grandmother's cake, Jake's layers wouldn't be so sweet. The thought gave her an unexpected thrill. What had he asked her? Something about danger?

"Tell me about your bad relationship that ended two years ago, the reason you came up with this charade." Jake's words hovered in the night air.

"Why do you want to know?"

He gripped her shoulders and pulled her around to face him, then held her in the circle of his arms. "A man hurt you, and it wasn't Steven. You say you don't want to get married but you concocted this whole lie for your family. Tell me about the man behind this."

When she shivered, he gathered her closer. Held in Jake's arms, Graceann felt secure and safe. She didn't want to think what that meant. The holidays would be over soon and they'd go their separate ways. The thought of not seeing him again sent an arrow of regret through her.

Taking a calming breath, she lifted her face to meet his eyes. "His name was Michael, and I fell head over heels for him the first time I met him. He was handsome, smart, witty, polished. He drove a Lamborghini and dressed in designer clothes. He completely swept me off my feet."

Jake stiffened. If she didn't know better she'd think he was jealous.

"You're not as superficial as that, Graceann. There had to be more to this guy. What type work did he do?"

"He was a financial wizard who worked on Wall Street. In fact, Zach introduced us. Zach thought we'd be good together. He didn't know the real Michael either."

"Who was the real Michael?"

"A serial cheater and pathological liar. Michael lied even when he didn't have to. Because of his looks and his money, he had women chasing him all the time. He rarely said no to them."

Remnants of the pain Michael had caused her twisted like a knife in her chest. She'd gotten over him, yet his betrayal had cut her deeply.

"Don't blame yourself." Jake kissed the top of her head. "Go on. I know there's more."

"There is. He asked me to marry him. I was so excited and happy. My family loved him. My mom was over the moon. I sometimes wonder which impressed her more, Michael's resume or the three-carat diamond he gave me. It wasn't long after we became engaged that I had a visitor to my table at a craft show." She chewed her lip. "And everything fell apart."

"A visitor?"

"A beautiful woman. She told me a jarring story."

Graceann blinked back tears at the memory. "I didn't believe her. I got someone to watch my table and I went outside to confront her with her lies. She told me everything—about Michael's other girlfriends, of which there were many, the way he spent money on them. She said he was marrying me because I was respectable and from a good family. I'd be an asset to his climb up the career ladder." Graceann grimaced. "Not the only time I've heard that one."

Remembered humiliation rolled through her and she rested her hands on Jake's upper arms, as if bracing herself to be pummeled anew by the devastating news she'd learned that day. "I defended him until I couldn't, until she hit me with the worst of it."

Jake hugged her close. "It's okay, Graceann. You don't have to tell me any more if it hurts too much."

Swiping at tears, she stepped back. "I want to tell you. This woman, her name was Kristin, was Michael's common-law wife. She lived in New Jersey with his two kids."

"He had kids and a woman stashed away in Jersey?" Anger radiated from Jake, so strong it hung between them like a black storm cloud.

Graceann nodded. "She said she loved Michael. They'd been high school sweethearts. When she got pregnant at eighteen, he refused to marry her. They lived together and had another child. But he still wouldn't marry her."

"Yet she stayed with him?" Jake asked.

"She said she loved him."

"That's not love. That's a lack of self-respect."

"I agree." Graceann gripped his arms again. "Michael had told her I was malleable, that he could do whatever he wanted after we were married and I wouldn't question him. So he would continue to support her and the kids while married to me. What a fool I was. But Michael was wrong about one thing. I'm not malleable and I wasn't about to stay with him."

"Baby, I'm sorry." Jake gathered her to him.

His heart beat strong and steady under her cheek, comforting and safe. Funny that The Falcon could make her feel so protected.

She pulled away and looked up at him. He watched her with eyes filled with understanding. "I'm okay now. I broke up with him right away. But I really feel sorry for Kristin and I think about her from time to time. I hope she comes to her senses and leaves that jerk."

Jake chuckled and brushed a light kiss on Graceann's lips. "Only you could worry about your ex-boyfriend's mistress. Proof of your sweetness and your adorableness. Don't ever change."

"Jake, I keep telling you I'm not really that sweet."

"Baby, you don't get it. You're the whole package—smart, caring, beautiful, and hot as hell."

He pressed his lips to hers in an urgent kiss that electrified every part of her body and touched something deep in her soul. His kiss coaxed and teased, urging her to give more, to give herself completely. An ache built between her thighs as she wound her arms around his neck and melted into him, opening her mouth to his hot invasion, letting him know she was his for the taking.

Consumed by her need, she moaned deep in her throat as her hands fumbled with the leather cord holding back his hair. She untied the cord and dropped it, then tunneled her fingers through his hair, craving naked skin next to naked skin, his hair brushing her bare chest.

He rained kisses along her neck. Then, cupping her face, he stared into her eyes. "I want you, Graceann."

Her heart pounded. "Jake, I—"

"Graceann! Jake! Come quick!" Her father's harried voice reached them and they pulled apart.

"Something's wrong," she said, her emotions an untidy mix of fear, frustration, and relief. True, she wanted Jake, but what did she really know about him?

All she knew was she was grateful for the strong, solid grip of his hand as he held hers while they ran to the house where her father waited by the back door, a worried look on his face. The sound of approaching sirens pierced the night air.

"What's wrong?" Graceann asked.

"It's your grandmother. We think she's having a heart attack."

Chapter Ten

AT SIX THE NEXT MORNING, Graceann and Jake trudged wearily up the walk to her grandmother's house after spending the night at the hospital. Graceann's parents were still with Grandmom.

As they slipped through the door and walked into the foyer, Lorrie, who'd stayed home with Andrew, Steven, and the kids, ran down the stairs. "You two look exhausted. Go upstairs and rest. We'll keep the kids quiet." She released a deep breath. "Thank God Grandmom's going to be okay."

Graceann rubbed a hand over her face. Her muscles screamed with fatigue. "I'm so glad it was only indigestion, but when you're in your late eighties the doctors can't take any chances."

"When are Mom and Dad bringing her home?"

"The hospital said they'd release her about noon."

Fluffy ran down the stairs, quiet for a change, and looked around. He began to whimper. Graceann bent to scratch him behind the ears. "You miss her, don't you, Fluffy? She'll be home soon."

"Come with me, Fluffy," Lorrie said. "I have a treat for you in the kitchen." The dog obediently followed her.

Graceann stood and Jake put his arm around her shoulders. "That dog must really miss your grandmother. He didn't try to bite me."

"He doesn't try to bite you."

"Yes, he does. The dog hates me."

She laughed. "No, he doesn't."

He gave her shoulder a gentle squeeze. "You see the good in everyone, even an annoying little dog." He grinned down at her as she smothered a yawn. "It's been a rough night. You need to rest."

"So do you."

"Don't worry about me. I wasn't an emotional ball of nerves until the good news came. Let's get you upstairs for some quality sleep."

When they reached her bedroom door, Jake took her in his arms and kissed her tenderly. She pulled away and skimmed a finger down his face. "Thanks for staying with me at the hospital. You didn't have to. I could have come home with Mom, Dad, and Grandmom."

He smiled. "How would it look if your fiancé selfishly abandoned you at the hospital?"

"Once you commit to a role, you really live the part, don't you?"

He silenced her with another soft kiss. "When I'm hired for a job I always deliver. Now get in there and get some sleep."

Graceann watched him as he strode with his customary lithe grace along the hallway to his room. Jake Falco was a very complex and caring guy once you looked under the surface. Smiling, she slipped into her room.

Nightgown on, she was ready to sink into her bed when a light knock sounded at her door. Heart thumping in anticipation of seeing Jake, she threw on her robe and opened the door. Her heart tumbled with disappointment when she saw Steven standing there.

She pulled her robe tighter. "What is it, Steven? I'm getting ready to take a nap."

"May I come in?"

Unsmiling, she gave him a level look. "No."

"I won't touch you. I promise. I need to say something."

With a sigh of resignation, she let him in, but was careful to keep the door open. Arms folded across her chest, she said, "Okay, start talking."

He smoothed a hand over his short hair. "I still love you, Graceann. I want to marry you. Your family wants that, too. Drop this jerk you're with and come back to me."

She took a step away. "You're the jerk, Steven. I can't believe we were even friends. I'm with Jake and it's where I want to be." As she said the words, she knew they were true. She wanted to be with Jake.

Steven grasped her shoulders. "You belong with me. You belong *to* me."

Breathing heavily, she jerked free and flung an arm toward the door. "Get out of my room and get out of this house. Now."

He stood there with a calculating expression on his hardened face.

"If you don't leave this minute, I'm going to scream. Jake and Andrew are here and they'll come running."

He backed toward the door. "I won't give up. That long-haired grease monkey isn't for you."

"Jake's twice the man you'll ever be. Get out."

His eyes like thunder clouds, Steven stormed out of her room and down the hall to his room.

She closed her door, leaned against it, and pressed a hand to her quaking belly. Funny how she once thought she might be in love with Steven. Everything about him paled in comparison to Jake. Jake liked to tease her but he was never mean. She couldn't see him acting as boorishly as Steven. Her mother had inadvertently done Jake a favor by inviting Steven. She'd allowed Graceann, and hopefully the rest of the family, to see Jake had something Steven didn't—depth and character.

As she slipped into bed, the realization hit her that she thought of Jake as a real fiancé. When had that happened? Before she could figure it out, she drifted off to sleep dreaming of Jake.

Later, the sound of voices woke Graceann. Yawning, she rolled over and looked at the clock. One. She'd slept for over five hours. That was enough. She'd never get back to sleep anyway.

She took a quick shower, pulled her hair into a ponytail, threw on a sweater and jeans—and her glasses—shoved her feet into her comfy moccasins, then headed down the back stairs. When she entered the kitchen, she found Lorrie, Andrew, and Jake seated around the center counter drinking coffee.

Like a heat-seeking missile, she zeroed in on Jake. He threw her a smile that lit up his face and made her throat go dry. "Afternoon, sunshine," he said, getting up from his stool and walking slowly toward her. He took her hand and pulled her to a stool. "Sit. I'll get you a cup of coffee. Do you want anything to eat? Lorrie makes a mean pumpkin bread."

"Thanks, Jake," Lorrie said. "I'm glad you like my pumpkin bread." A blush spread over her face.

Andrew shot his wife a narrow-eyed look that made Graceann stifle a grin.

"I love Lorrie's pumpkin bread," Graceann said, starting to rise from her stool.

Jake shook his head. "You stay there, princess, and I'll wait on you."

Lorrie sighed. "Jake, you spoil her."

He chuckled. "And I intend to keep doing it."

Graceann widened her eyes at Jake. He winked at her, then strolled to the coffeemaker. She wondered when she'd lost control of the situation.

"Steven left in a hurry," Lorrie said. "Did you have anything to do with that?"

Graceann shrugged and feigned innocence. "I guess he thought with everything going on now, it would be best for him to leave." She frowned when Jake nearly knocked over the pitcher with the creamer. What happened was between her and Steven. Wasn't it?

If Jake knew anything, he wasn't saying.

Then neither was she. "Is Grandmom home yet?" she asked her sister.

Lorrie nodded. "They got in about a half hour ago. They're all resting. Even Fluffy. He won't leave Grandmom's side. Other than being tired, she seems back to her old self."

"That's good."

As Graceann was finishing her third cup of coffee and her second piece of pumpkin bread, a loud wail coming from the second floor shattered the silence.

"Isabella," Lorrie said, pushing away from the counter. "She's going to wake everyone. I hoped she'd sleep longer. All the Christmas excitement, I guess."

"Stay here," Andrew said to Lorrie. "I'll get Isabella." He jumped up and jogged to the stairs.

Lorrie sank back onto her stool as her look of gratitude followed Andrew from the room and up the stairs.

Graceann cradled her mug and inhaled the sweet aroma of hazelnut. "Jake and I can take Izzie off your hands for a while to give you a break."

"Sure," Jake said. "Why not? Would you mind if we took her outside to build a snowman?"

Lorrie looked at them as if they'd morphed into two of Santa's more unlikely elves. "Do you know what you're saying? She's a handful."

Jake chuckled. "She won't be a problem." He looked toward Graceann. "Right, sweetheart?"

She gave him her sweetest smile. "That's right, *darling.*"

Dressed for the outdoors, Jake waited by the front door with Graceann for Lorrie to bring Isabella. Graceann leaned in to whisper to him. "You were really laying it on thick back there in the kitchen."

She looked so adorably self-righteous with her eyes flashing. He suppressed a laugh, knowing even a smile would get him a punch in the arm. Giving her what he hoped was an innocent look, he said, "I want to spoil you, *sweetheart.*"

"I'm not you're sweetheart, *angel.*"

"Who says you're not?"

Before Graceann could answer, Lorrie came down the stairs holding a bundled-up Isabella. When she got to the bottom step, she let the little girl down. Isabella waddled over to Graceann and held out her arms. Laughing, Graceann picked her up. "You can barely move in all these clothes, sweetie." She kissed Isabella on her cheek.

"I don't want her to catch cold," Lorrie said.

"She can't move enough to catch a snowflake," Graceann said.

Lorrie shrugged.

Jake opened the door. "Let's go build that snowman."

Later, a giggling Isabella helped Jake and Graceann roll a huge snowball into place for the base of the snowman. The little girl was covered with snow. "You look like a snowman yourself," Jake said. Isabella giggled louder.

Graceann knelt to brush snow off Isabella's coat and adjust the little girl's hat. At the picture of maternal love, Jake reeled with unexpected longing. Fragments of memories rose in him like spirits arising from a mist—his mother adjusting his hat in the same way Graceann fixed Isabella's; his mother holding him against her chest in a tender embrace. When he was small, his mom always wore rose-scented perfume. Even now the scent of roses reminded him of her. He had so few memories of loving times with his mother. Too soon, the roses were replaced by the stench of alcohol.

Uneasy with his painful trip down memory lane, Jake gathered snow and molded it between his hands until he had a perfectly formed ball. Today was a time for fun, the kind of fun he barely remembered with his own parents. He readied his arm for the pitch.

Finished with the little girl's hat, Graceann stood. Her eyes grew wide when she saw the snowball. "Oh, no, you don't," she said, laughing. She scooped up a clump of snow to throw at him, but he was too fast. His snowball hit her in the shoulder.

Before he could throw another one, she quickly formed a ball and threw it, hitting him in the arm.

Laughing, Isabella danced around them. "Me, me!" she shouted.

"Over here, Izzie," Graceann said. "Girls against the guy."

"I'm outnumbered," Jake said in mock fright.

The intense snowball fight was the most fun Jake had had in more years than he could remember. His leather jacket was covered with snow, but he didn't care. He deliberately took a very long time making each snowball to give the females, especially Isabella, ample time to pummel him.

Graceann and Isabella's laughter tinkled in the clear air, a happy, carefree sound that shot an unfamiliar feeling of joy to his heart. With a saucy smile for him, Graceann handed Isabella a perfectly formed snowball to throw. His chest tightened. Graceann had never looked more sweet than she did at this moment, with her thick hair flying around her face and her cheeks pink from the cold. Her full lips—.

He had no more time to think as Isabella's snowball hit him in the heart. Clutching his chest, Jake fell onto the snow. Isabella squealed with delight. The females high-fived each other.

Jake's laughter joined theirs. No matter what happened between him and Graceann, this Christmas with the Palmer family would go down as his happiest ever. A tinge of sorrow wrapped around him with the realization of all he'd missed in his life. Real families had fun together. Real families loved each other.

Graceann signaled him the fight was over and stooped to pick up the little girl. "You're tired, aren't you, sweetie?" Isabella wound her arms around Graceann's neck and snuggled close.

As Jake stood, Graceann raised her gaze to his. Something passed between them then, something vibrant and pulsing and filled with promise. His breathing slowed. A vision of him and Graceann together, of her holding their child, wavered before him. He couldn't move, couldn't look away.

"We'd better go in," Graceann said.

The moment was lost. Shaking his head, he said, "Take Isabella in then come back out. We haven't finished yet. We promised her a snowman."

Dusk was settling around them as they finished building their snowman. Graceann and Jake stood back and studied their work. They'd dressed their creation in an old fedora and a red scarf Lorrie had found in the house.

"Looks damn good," he said. "That's one of the handsomest snowmen I've ever seen. We need to take his picture."

"We're artists," Graceann said.

He turned to her. "You're the artist. You're the one who designed him. I'm the laborer following your orders. Very few people could do what you do with jewelry. Or with snowmen."

Smiling, she took a bow. "Thank you, Jake."

Her smile chipped away a little more of the wall around his heart. "I like your family." His words came out unbidden. "I always figured close families were dull, but your family's cool. I didn't believe parents and siblings could love each other. But you all do."

She slipped off a glove and reached out to touch his face. "Oh, Jake."

He wanted to take her into his arms and never let her go. But he didn't want her pity. Deliberately breaking their tender connection, he stepped back and gave her a wicked grin. Her gaze traveled to the arm he held at his side. A huge snowball rested in the palm of his gloved hand.

"Oh, no." She began to run away.

The snowball hit the middle of her back, then he tackled her. They rolled on the soft snow-packed ground together. When they'd settled, she lay on her back with him on top of her. He propped himself up on his elbows.

Her pupils were dilated. "No fair," she said. "I wasn't ready to fight." Her words came out on a husky breath.

"Are you ready for this?"

He took her sweet lips in a kiss that poured out his need for her, a need that grew stronger every day. She wrapped her arms around his neck and pulled him down. He slid his tongue along her lips. She opened to him. She tasted of coffee and mint. His body on fire, he wondered why the snow around them didn't melt.

When his hard erection pressed against her stomach, she moaned into his mouth. Her passion fueled his hunger. He kissed her harder and deeper, as if he could devour her.

"Dinner's ready, you two!" Lorrie's high-pitched voice coming from the opened front door was the most unwelcome sound he'd heard in a long while.

Jake slowly pulled away and stared down at Graceann. Happiness and desire flashed in her eyes. "You are amazing," he whispered.

"So are you." She cupped his face. "You're wonderful."

He froze. Him, wonderful? "You've been out in the cold too long."

Dinner was an informal affair around the kitchen counter. Lorrie had taken a tray of food up to their grandmother. After they'd had their coffee and dessert, Graceann stood and pushed her stool away. "Is it okay for Grandmom to have dessert? She loves apple pie."

Her mother nodded. "The doctor said she can eat anything but to watch her portions. And she can't have coffee for a while."

"Good," Graceann said. "I'll bring dessert and tea to her. I haven't seen her since she got back from the hospital."

Graceann knocked softly on her grandmother's door, then pushed it open. The older woman was sitting up in bed watching TV. Her tray with the empty dinner dishes was on the nightstand. Fluffy was curled up close to her. The dog lifted its head when Graceann opened the door, then with a yawn, went back to sleep.

A fire snapped in the fireplace, heating the room and filling it with the acrid aroma of burning wood. Sweet memories stole over Graceann. She and Lorrie used to sit on either side of Grandmom on the bed while she read to them as a fire crackled in the hearth. Smiling, she walked into the room.

Grandmom returned her smile and muted the TV. Graceann set the dessert plate and the tea mug on the tray next to the dinner dishes, then leaned over to give her grandmother a hug.

"You look good, Grandmom." She settled onto the bed and held one of her grandmother's hands.

"I do not look good." The older woman touched her hair with her free hand. "I have bed head."

Graceann laughed. "So you have a little bed head. You're still beautiful."

Her grandmother's face lit in another smile. "You always know the right thing to say. Where's that handsome fiancé of yours? I watched out the window as you two built the snowman." She gave her a sly grin. "I saw the snowball fight, too."

Had her grandmother seen them kiss? Graceann's face felt hot and she knew she blushed. "You shouldn't have been out of bed."

Grandmom waved a hand. "I'm fine. Everyone coddles me." She shifted, and Graceann fluffed her pillow behind her. Settling back, the older woman studied Graceann. "I like Jake very much." She stroked Fluffy's head. "Fluffy likes him, too."

"I'm not sure 'like' is the right word for what Fluffy feels toward Jake."

"I know my dog. He's a good judge of character. He likes Jake. So, did you and Jake set a date yet?"

Graceann looked toward the window as guilt choked her.

"What is it, child?" her grandmother asked. "Something's bothering you."

Graceann faced her grandmother and kissed her on the cheek. Grandmom's skin felt paper-thin. Swiping at a tear, Graceann took a steadying breath. "I was afraid we'd lost you. I don't know what we'd do without you."

Grandmom snorted. "I plan to live to 100 or beyond. By the time I go, you'll be glad to be rid of me. But there's something else bothering you. 'Fess up."

Graceann blew out a breath. "I was afraid you'd die not knowing the truth about Jake and me. I don't know if I could have lived with that guilt."

"What are you trying to say?" Grandmom's brow furrowed.

"If I tell you something, promise you won't tell anyone, especially Mom and Daddy." She squeezed her grandmother's hand.

"That depends on what it is."

"Promise me. Please."

"I promise since it clearly means so much to you."

She rubbed her grandmother's hand, gathering her thoughts, then raised her gaze. "Jake and I aren't engaged. I hired him to be my pretend fiancé through the holidays."

When Grandmom stared at her without saying a word, dread settled like a tight knot in Graceann's chest.

"Why would you do that?" her grandmother asked at last.

"You know how Mom is always trying to fix me up with some guy. Look at how she invited Steven here. She feels sorry for me and she won't listen when I tell her I'm over Michael and I'm doing fine on my own."

"Your mother means well. She and your father want you to be happy."

"I know. But I am happy. I have my work, which I love. I have friends. I have New York City. I have an active social life."

"Your parents want to see you settled like your sister, with a dependable family man like Andrew."

"Lorrie's happy, and I'm happy for her. Maybe I'll get married someday, but I'm in no hurry." The snap of the fire caught her attention and she looked over. She watched the blaze flicker and sputter as her words tumbled out, as wavering and unsteady as the flames. "I'm not sure I want to get married, but I do want children. I'd have to get married to have them. That's the way I was raised. Why can't Mom accept that I'm capable of finding my own man and living my own life?" She turned back to her grandmother.

"I understand, dear. I want to see you happy, too. And I'd like more great-grandchildren before I go."

Graceann kissed the older woman's cheek again. "I know, but please let me do what I want in my own time and my own way."

"Who is Jake, really?" her grandmother asked.

"I went to school with him. He was a couple of years ahead of me. I—I'm paying him to act the part of my fiancé."

Grandmom raised an eyebrow. "Paying him?"

"It sounds tawdry when you say it like that, but it's strictly a business arrangement."

"I see." She sank into a thoughtful pause. "Does Jake really repair motorcycles?"

Graceann chewed her lip. "I don't know what type work he does."

Grandmom raised both eyebrows this time. "You don't know what he does, yet you trust him enough to bring him into my house, to meet the family?"

"I do trust him." The words slipped out. "He's a decent man."

"And you're in love with him."

127

Her grandmother's quiet words jolted Graceann. "No, I'm not. I like him, that's all."

"Child." She smiled and patted Graceann's hand. "I've been around a long time. I recognize when two people are in love. Jake loves you, too. I watched you together outside building the snowman, chasing each other. You're in love."

"Don't say that. Please. After the holidays, I'll pay Jake and he'll go back to wherever he lives and I'll never see him again." Sadness tightened the knot in her chest.

"I don't believe that's what you want. You want him to stay."

"I admit I've gotten close to him these last few days, and I might miss him a little, but life goes on and I'll move onto other things and so will he."

The older woman studied her. "Whatever you say, dear. I promise not to breathe a word to your parents, but how will you handle Jake's exit from your life?"

"I'll tell them I broke up with him. That he didn't want to break up but I decided he wasn't the guy I wanted to marry after all. They'll stop feeling sorry for me because of Michael and realize I'm in control of my life. Then Mom will quit trying to marry me off to guys like the dentist who couldn't keep his hands to himself." She shuddered. "Or the guy who called his mother five times during our dinner date.

And she'll quit inviting Steven to spend family time with us."

Grandmom laughed. "You don't know your mother. Nothing will deter her in her quest to see both her girls happily married."

Stubbornly, Graceann shook her head. "My plan will work. I know it will. Remember your promise."

"Something tells me things won't work out exactly as you've planned," her grandmother said. "Life has a way of throwing us curves."

Chapter Eleven

THE NEXT MORNING Graceann sat in the kitchen having a breakfast of English muffin, jam and coffee. All except her mom and Jake were there. Isabella held court from her highchair, getting more cereal on her than in her. Graceann let her gaze linger on her niece and sister. In between sips of coffee, Lorrie wiped the milk off Isabella's face and tried, but failed, to keep her highchair tray clean. Graceann smiled at the homey picture her sister presented.

Footsteps on the back stairs snatched her attention and she focused on the doorway. Jake, dressed in a sweater, jeans, boots, and his leather jacket strode in and deposited his duffel bag on the floor. She and Jake hadn't had a chance to be alone again last night. But her sleeping hours had been filled with erotic dreams of him. She'd woken in a state of frustration, her body tight with need.

Seeing him dressed for the outdoors and carrying his duffel, Graceann's heart sank. He was leaving.

"Where are you going?" she asked him.

"Morning to you, too," he said with a smile. He looked around at the others. "Morning, everyone."

The others mumbled their greetings.

Fluffy, at his food bowl, looked up, then ran at Jake and began barking.

"Fluffy, stop it," her dad said.

With one more bark at Jake, Fluffy trotted back to his food.

"You're leaving?" Lorrie asked with a frown.

Jake met Graceann's gaze. "Work called. I need to go away for a few days. I've ordered a car. I have time to grab a cup of coffee first."

"I'll make one for you," Grandmom said. "It'll be ready in a minute."

He smiled at her. "Thanks." Then he turned to Graceann. "Can we talk? In private?"

Nodding, Graceann rose.

Jake held Graceann's elbow and led her into the entry hall, far enough from the kitchen so no one could hear them.

Once they were alone, she pulled free, and rubbing her arms, faced him. "Why are you leaving now, of all times? I'm paying you to be here for the entire holiday." Her voice came out harsher than she'd intended, but she couldn't let him know she didn't care about the holiday or what she was paying him. She'd grown close to him these last few days and she didn't want him to go.

He smoothed a hand over his hair. "I know. I wouldn't go if it wasn't important. I'll only be away a few days. Something came up." His expression sobered. "I never intended to take your money."

She stepped back. "You didn't?"

"No, but that's not important now."

"I think it is. But we'll discuss it later because the most important thing at the moment is my mom's New Year's Eve party. I need you here for that."

"I'll be back in plenty of time. I promise." He pulled her to him and looked deeply into her eyes. "Money or no money, I never go back on my word. Trust me. Please."

She'd told her grandmother she trusted Jake. Yet, apprehension settled like a ball of ice in her chest. If Jake walked away and never came back, the humiliation would haunt her for years. And her mom would never stop trying to marry her off to some jerk. She stared into his face as he held her gaze.

"All right, but where are you going?" she asked.

"Not far. I'll be in the area. I'm not at liberty to say much now, but I'll tell you all about it as soon as I can."

"You're not into anything illegal, are you?"

He flinched as if hit. "Do you have so little faith in me?"

Knowing she'd hurt him and suddenly realizing it was because of her own fear of being hurt by him, she touched his arm in apology. The leather of his jacket was smoother and softer than it looked. This was no ordinary motorcycle jacket, but something much more expensive. Another mystery. She shoved the realization aside. She needed Jake to return for New Year's Eve.

"I've gotten to know you well," she said quietly. "And I don't believe you'd be into something illegal, but you've got to admit you're awfully mysterious."

"I'm not hiding anything dark. I swear to that. I like to keep things close to my chest. And I'm a tad superstitious. I don't want to jinx something by talking about it."

She studied him. She would take him at his word. What choice did she have? "Better drink that coffee before your ride gets here."

As she followed him back to the kitchen, she told herself everything would be okay. But the apprehension that lay heavy in her chest wouldn't melt.

Jake settled into the luxurious back seat of the town car. Nervousness had him feeling like a green kid just out of film school. He hadn't expected his partner to find potential backers so soon. They'd pitched the original story arc, and that's what the backers were interested in. After spending time with Graceann and her family, Jake knew he had to make adjustments to his story. He had ideas percolating in his mind, ideas he believed made the story better. He needed to sell it to his partner along with the backers.

Hard as he tried to focus on the upcoming meeting, his thoughts kept winding back to Graceann. Maybe he should have been upfront with her from the beginning. Yet, he held back. First, she'd offered him money. Now, she thought he might be into something illegal. She still couldn't separate him from the mixed-up kid he'd been. He'd left that kid behind the day he'd hopped on his chopper carrying the money he'd earned from his after-school job, money he'd hidden from his parents, and made his way cross-country.

Each day he spent with Graceann made him more determined to show her the real man behind the laid-back façade. He'd known his share of women who wanted him only because of his connections in the industry, who didn't care to delve too deeply into Jake Falco. He wanted so much more from Graceann.

The picturesque countryside rolled past. It should have soothed, but it didn't. His mind was awhirl, filled with Graceann and the dilemma in which he found himself. He needed to focus. This meeting was too important to blow. Forcing his thoughts back to the meeting, he rehearsed his pitch.

She missed him. And she was annoyed. Tomorrow was New Year's Eve, and Jake hadn't returned. As much as Graceann tried to deny it, the minute Jake left three days ago, a void had opened in her heart. He'd begun to mean much more to her than a fiancé-of-convenience.

The thought scared her to death.

Standing at the counter in the butler's pantry, she completed the mindless task of polishing one of Grandmom's silver tea services. They wouldn't be using it at the New Year's Eve party, but her mom had insisted on polishing it so she could display it on one of the two sideboards in the dining room. The housekeeper had polished the smaller silver set before she took off for the holidays, but Graceann's mother had changed her mind and decided she wanted to use the larger one.

The more Graceann thought of Jake and how much she missed him, the harder she rubbed the sugar bowl. If it were a genie's lamp, the genie would have been out by now and she'd have her three wishes. She could use a little magic to bring Jake back soon, before the party, before she went crazy with missing him.

Where was he? He'd called her every day, though they were rushed calls to say hello. She always heard others speaking in the background, but Jake didn't offer where he was. Damn cell phones. Much as she loved them, a person could be calling from anywhere in the world.

Jake had called her every night, too, as she was getting ready for bed. Those calls were longer, with enough sexual innuendos and tension bouncing between them to melt her phone.

Giving the sugar bowl a few last wipes, she set it back on the tray, her thoughts still on Jake. She needed time alone without silver bowls and party-obsessed mothers. And she needed to discuss her fears and her growing feelings for Jake with someone. She couldn't talk to Lorrie without divulging her deception. Kate was still in Philadelphia with her boyfriend's family but promised to be at the party tomorrow. She'd talked with Kate a few times by phone since the holidays began, but there were some things that needed saying in person. Her confusion about Jake was one of those things.

"Graceann, are you finished yet?" Her mother's voice startled her.

"Be right out." Straightening, she mustered her courage to face her mom, or rather Angie Palmer, drill sergeant. Yesterday, a cleaning crew had given the house a good going-over. But her perfectionist mom had enlisted everyone in the family to help with extra cleaning and arranging and rearranging the furniture to accommodate the eighty people expected at the party. The Palmer family's New Year's Eve party had grown through the years from a quiet gathering of friends to a catered, elegant event.

As much as Graceann loved the annual party, the days leading up to it were always fraught with tension as her mom made everyone around her crazy with her insistence on perfection. Even Grandmom had gone into hiding, taking Fluffy with her.

Graceann found her mother bent over the center counter in the kitchen, intently entering notes into her tablet. Her mom kept copious notes on each year's party. "What's up, Mom?"

"The catering people will be here any minute." Her mom didn't look up. "I need help directing them to where I want the tables set up. Your father and Andrew went to the hardware store hours ago to get some tools. I don't know what kind of tools they needed so desperately they had to run out now."

Graceann suppressed a grin. She knew her dad and Andrew had wanted an excuse to escape. She didn't blame them. "Stop worrying, Mom. Your party is a success every year. This year will be the same. Everything will work out. It always does."

The doorbell rang, making both women jump. "That must be the caterers with the tables," her mom said.

"I'll get the door." Graceann hurried out.

She flung open the front door and gasped. Jake stood there, looking a little tired, with a few days' growth of stubble on his face. She'd never seen a more beautiful sight.

"You're back." Her words tumbled out on a shaky breath.

He stepped inside and gathered her to him, holding her tight. "God, I missed you," he whispered. He buried his face in her hair.

She clung to him, inhaling his pine-laced scent of the outdoors. He'd come back to her.

He kissed her throat and worked his way up to her mouth. "I can't believe how much I missed you," he said against her lips. Then his lips captured hers in a kiss that told her the truth of his words.

She opened to him, giving herself freely. She didn't care who saw them, didn't care that Jake might guess how much he was coming to mean to her. All she cared about was that he was here, now, with her.

"Graceann, is that the tables?" Her mother's voice shattered the moment.

Graceann and Jake pulled apart.

Angie walked into the foyer. "Jake, you're back. Just in time. We need all the help we can get."

A confused expression on his face, Jake looked at Graceann. She laughed. "You'll probably wish you'd stayed away a little longer. We're in full party mode."

He put his arm around her waist. "I couldn't stay away longer. I had to get back to you."

"Tell me when they come with the tables. I'll be in the kitchen." Angie made a quick exit.

Graceann smiled at Jake. "If you value your sanity, do whatever Mom tells you."

"That sounds ominous," he said with a laugh.

"It is. How did your, uh, business meeting go?"

"Good. Probably could have been better. They didn't show their cards so I couldn't get a read on what they're thinking."

"You want to tell me about it?"

"I want to tell you, but I can't yet. Still unsure of things and I don't want to jinx myself. I will tell you soon. I promise. If I don't get backing for my project, there won't be much to tell anyway."

Disappointment worked its way through her. She trusted Jake, but he didn't seem to trust her enough to tell her where he'd been for the last three days. Backing? Project? What kind of business was he in?

The doorbell rang again and she had no more time to dwell on Jake's reason for being away. While the catering crew delivered the tables, Lorrie came downstairs after having put the kids down for their naps. Her dad and Andrew strolled in a little later. They admitted they'd stopped at the local pub while out.

Lorrie sidled up to Andrew and said, "Coward."

The next hours were spent in a flurry of activity. The men put up New Year's party decorations while the women directed the caterers to set up the tables and rearrange the furniture again. As they worked, Graceann's mother floated around like a butterfly on steroids. Finally the tables were placed to her satisfaction and covered with white linen tablecloths. Tomorrow morning the florist would bring the flower arrangements for all the rooms on the first floor.

After dinner and some TV watching the family called it an early night. Jake followed Graceann up the stairs. They hadn't had a chance to talk since he'd gotten back. They stopped at the door to her room, and he took her into his arms and held her close. Feeling secure and peaceful, she rested her head on his chest.

"Your mother is a whirlwind, isn't she?" he said.

"When it comes to her New Year's Eve party, yes."

"Do you think she likes me any better now that Steven is gone?"

"She likes you." She pulled back to look at him. "She recruited you to help out with the party preparations." Graceann chuckled. "She only lets family touch those decorations. Does it matter to you what she thinks?"

He shrugged. "A little. But I understand if she can't accept me. I'm not exactly marriage material."

She placed a finger over his lips. "Don't sell yourself short. You can't fool me. You're a dependable guy."

He blinked and looked at her with hooded eyes. Then his lips tilted in a teasing grin. "I must be a better actor than I thought. See you in the morning."

She nodded, then watched as he walked down the hall with the lithe grace that always caused her heart to thump a little louder.

A half hour later, she'd showered and put on her nightgown. As she brushed out her hair in front of the mirror, she felt restless, needy. Her body thrummed with pent-up energy. She stopped brushing in mid-stroke and stared at her reflection. She knew what she wanted, what she had to do.

Chapter Twelve

GRACEANN KNOCKED ON Jake's bedroom door. He opened it and peered out. When he saw her, his face broke into a smile and he opened the door wider, beckoning her in.

"To what do I owe this pleasure?" he asked when she'd slipped inside.

She licked her lips as her hungry gaze scanned him. His hair was pulled back as usual but damp as if he'd just gotten out of the shower and he was clean-shaven. Dressed only in his jeans, his chest bare, his masculine beauty made her breath hitch. His broad chest with taut, sharply defined muscles and a scattering of black hairs tapered to six-pack abs. She followed the line of hair leading past the waistband of his jeans. Her mouth went dry.

Jake closed the door and leaned against it. The glint in his eyes made her take a step back. Maybe she should have thought this whole thing through.

"Graceann, what are you doing here?"

She pulled the sash on her robe tighter, as if she could rein in her desire for him. "I, uh, I couldn't sleep."

"There's a lot of that going around." He moved closer. "Is there something you want?"

"Yes," she managed.

"Is this what you want?" He skimmed his fingers down her throat, along her chest to the hollow between her breasts.

"Yes." The word floated out on a whisper.

Liquid fire raced through her veins when he loosened the sash on her robe and slipped it off her. She stood before him clad only in her short, sheer nightgown and a red thong.

He drew her close. "You're sure?"

"More sure than I've ever been about anything." She reached out a hand to cup the curve of his jaw. "I want you, Jake."

His lips met hers, hard and demanding. This time there was no gentleness, no hesitation. His kiss told her how much he wanted her. She wound her arms around his neck and twined her tongue with his in an erotic dance.

Still kissing her, he slipped her nightgown off her shoulders. She dropped her arms to let the soft silk slide down her body.

He stepped back, his breathing labored. "A thong? I would have expected demure white panties. Damn, you're sexy as hell and full of surprises."

"I've got more surprises in store for you."

"I can't wait." With a husky laugh, he stepped close again. His hands massaged and caressed her breasts as his mouth and tongue continued to assault her senses, driving her deeper and deeper into a pleasure-filled paradise where nothing existed but Jake.

He fisted his hand in her hair and tipped back her head, exposing her throat to his urgent kisses. Nipping and licking, he strung a line of hot kisses down her throat and chest to her breasts. He gently released her and knelt before her to slide her thong down her legs. She stepped out of the tiny piece of silk and kicked it aside. Pulling her closer, he kissed her stomach and dipped his tongue into her navel.

Graceann dug her fingers into Jake's shoulders, not sure her legs could hold her. Desire pulsed through her, making her tremble. She felt no worry, no anxiety, just a deep-seated need for this man. She wanted to melt into him, to become a part of him. Like a rare Christmas rose, Jake had slowly and seductively opened her to her full passion. Her newfound sexual boldness filled her with a mixture of delight and anxiety. She didn't question her feelings, but let them roll through her, blotting out all thought but the sensations his touch aroused.

He stood and took her hand, leading her to the

bed. He yanked the comforter aside. With a sigh, she sank onto the firm mattress. The soft cotton sheets cooled her heated flesh.

"Take off your clothes," she whispered.

He quickly shed his clothes until he stood before her, an Adonis come to claim his woman.

"You're beautiful," she breathed, as her gaze drank in his long legs, firm thighs and his erection—hard, thick, magnificent.

He stared down at her with smoldering eyes, tempting and seductive as a moon-kissed night. "I've wanted you for so long."

She held out her arms. "Love me, Jake."

Then he was on the bed beside her, holding her close. Her breasts pressed against his muscled chest. She'd dreamed of him like this, dreamed of feeling his naked skin against hers. She loosened the strip of leather that held back his hair, tossing the leather aside. His hair fell in silky disarray around his face, as she'd imagined. She squirmed at the sudden rush of warmth to her lower abdomen.

He took her lips again in a deep, drugging kiss. She reveled in his possession, in his masculine strength. Pressing her onto her back, he kissed a scorching trail down her body, scraping his teeth against her skin, licking where he'd kissed, his hair a seductive curtain teasing her sensitized flesh. When he kissed her mound, she grabbed handfuls of the sheets, writhing under him.

He didn't linger, but continued his carnal trip, kissing her inner thighs, running his hands down her calves. When he got to her ankles, he raised one of her legs and kissed the arch of her foot. The delicious feelings that stole over her ratcheted up her desire.

Then he worked his way back up her body with maddening slowness, worshiping her with his talented hands and mouth, driving her little-by-little toward the edge.

When he slipped a finger into her wet folds, she arched up, releasing a low growl of pleasure. He slipped in another finger, massaging her nub with his thumb. He kissed her as his fingers thrust in and out.

Her climax built like flaming waves crashing over her in a wild crescendo. She gripped the sheets harder as she came apart.

He gathered her trembling body in his arms and held her close until she stilled. "You okay?"

"Never better," she croaked out.

Laughing softly, he slipped from the bed and walked to his duffel bag on the floor by his closet. Graceann touched her breasts, rolling the puckered nipples between her fingers as her gaze followed him. He was a god, with his long back that tapered to a slim waist and firm buttocks. His thick black hair skimmed his shoulders, swaying enticingly.

He pulled something out of his duffel, then turned around, holding a box of condoms. He walked back, opening it to pull one out, then tossed the box onto the floor.

"You were confident," she teased.

He grinned wickedly. "I may not have been a boy scout, but I believe in being prepared."

He sat on the bed, pulled on protection, then took her into his arms again.

As they faced each other, a surge of heat shot through her. She smoothed a hand over the firm, smooth planes of his chest and slid one of her legs over his. His penis jerked against her thigh. She basked in his masculine scent of spice and soap.

His lips took hers in a fevered kiss. She moaned softly, her body boneless, on fire. She'd waited her whole life for this man, for this sensation of falling into his arms, of giving herself freely—body and soul.

He rolled her over and settled his hard-muscled body between her legs. His features were tight, his eyes dark. His hair swung around his face. "Graceann," he whispered in a voice harsh with need.

Then he thrust inside her, hard and fast, going deep. Gasping, she arched her hips and met his every thrust. She closed her eyes, letting the raw sensations of Jake's body claiming hers override all thought. There was no yesterday, no tomorrow. There was only now.

"Look at me," he growled.

What she saw in his eyes made her shudder with desire and hope. Lust was there, but so were other emotions—hunger, need, vulnerability—emotions that made her heart pump so fast she feared it might shoot out of her chest.

He threw back his head and plunged deeper into her, harder and faster. A raging firestorm built inside her. She wrapped her legs around his hips, wanting to fuse her body with his as the storm possessed her, taking her closer and closer to the precipice.

His skin was damp against hers. Nothing but the sheen of sweat separated them. Fire inflamed her every cell, burning out of control. She was all raw need, wanting only to taste Jake, to consume him. Her climax hit her with explosive force, and she came apart again. She clung to Jake as he drove his hips harder and harder, then shuddered with his own climax.

Spent, they lay entwined in each other's arms. Finally, the coolness of the room made her shiver. They slipped between the sheets and pulled the comforter over them.

He took her into his arms again and kissed her gently on the lips. "That was incredible. You're okay?"

She touched his face. "That was beyond incredible. I want to do it again."

He laughed. "Again? Give me a little time, sweetheart, then I'm all yours."

She snuggled close. "Promise?"

"Promise."

Jake stirred, then opened his eyes. The first light of dawn infused the bedroom in pale gray shadows. The memory of his night with Graceann brought him awake. He propped himself on his elbow and watched her as she slept next to him. Her chest rose and fell with her gentle breathing.

Her sable-colored hair spread over the pillow, and her long black lashes feathered her soft cheeks. The faint jasmine and sandalwood scent of her perfume mixed with the primitive scent of their lovemaking and tightened his body with a rush of desire. She looked sweet and innocent. Last night had proved, to his delighted surprise, she was far from innocent. Beneath her classy exterior beat the heart of a tigress, a hot, sexy woman with passion, imagination and a willingness to do whatever he wanted. She was unlike any woman he'd ever known.

He lay back down as guilt sucker-punched him in the gut. He should have told her the truth from the beginning, told her the real reason he'd come back to Spirit Lake. Fool that he was, he'd figured he could walk away from her without a backward glance. Graceann Palmer wasn't a woman a man walked away from with his soul intact. She was a forever kind of woman, but he'd never been a forever kind of man.

Jake rubbed a hand over his face. He was a love 'em and leave 'em type. Although, the past year he'd been so immersed in his writing and his various projects he hadn't time to love or leave any woman. Besides, love had little to do with his previous relationships. Yearning pounded through him, almost a physical ache, a longing to be the kind of man Graceann needed, maybe the kind of man he needed to be.

Guilt rose up again. Once he knew if they had backing for the project, he'd tell Graceann everything. His conscience eased a little. If she knew the truth, would she want him for himself, or for his public persona? She had to want him for who he truly was, without all the trappings. Anxiety settled in his chest again.

Beside him, Graceann slid closer, nestling her body against his. He turned on his side and looked at her. She opened her big green eyes, and he was lost.

"Morning," she whispered.

"Morning, princess." He leaned over her and kissed her softly.

She brushed hair back from his face. "I never knew long hair on a guy could be such a turn-on."

He chuckled and cupped her firm butt, pulling her closer. His burgeoning erection pressed against her soft skin. "Is that the only part of me that turns you on?"

"You have many fine, uh, qualities that turn me on."

"I never knew such a sweet princess could be so wild in bed."

Her sultry grin shot a fresh round of desire through him. "My days of being a sweet princess are over. You've turned me into a bad one." She wound a strand of his hair around her finger. "I like being a bad princess."

"Baby, I'm ready. Have your way with me."

Chapter Thirteen

THAT EVENING GRACEANN turned slowly in front of the full-length mirror in her room. She'd worn this body-hugging sleeveless black dress with the deep V-shaped neckline many times. It was one of her favorites. But tonight, she looked different. More vibrant, sexier. Her skin seemed to glow. Smiling, she ran a finger over her bottom lip, remembering Jake's mouth on hers, his teeth nipping her there.

They'd been so busy all day with party preparations that she and Jake had only had time to snatch a few minutes together. But while they worked getting the house as perfect as her mother demanded, she was aware of Jake whenever he was near. When they passed each other, they touched.

She needed the physical contact or she'd go mad. And from the way he looked at her, he felt the same. For the first time ever, her mother's stress barely registered. Graceann's mind was focused solely on Jake.

With a sigh, she walked over to her dresser and picked up her dangling peridot earrings, a college graduation gift from her parents. They and the matching necklace would complement the green silk shawl Jake had given her.

She'd hooked the earrings through her ears and reached for the necklace when a soft knock sounded at the door. Anticipating Jake, her pulse jumped. She opened the door to him.

"Wow, you look amazing," she said.

Wearing a charcoal gray suit, striped tie, snowy white shirt, and his black hair slicked back, he could have stepped from the pages of a men's fashion magazine. No one would think Jake unpolished tonight. Not that she cared. She wanted to devour him.

His eyes lit as his gaze made a slow, sexually-charged journey down her body and back to her face. "You look gorgeous…and hot."

"I'll show you hot." She grabbed him by his tie and pulled him into the room, then shoved the door closed and pulled his face down to hers. Gripping his shoulders, she kissed him with all the passion and wildness he'd unleashed in her. With a guttural moan, he cupped her buttocks and pressed her close until she felt his hard erection against her stomach.

Finally, breathing heavily, they pulled apart.

"Damn," he said, his voice shaky. "Let's stay here."

She laughed. "I wish, but we need to show up at the party. I'm almost ready. I have to put on my necklace."

"Let me do it." He followed her to the dresser, then picked up the large pear-shaped peridot stone surrounded by diamonds and strung on a delicate gold chain.

She faced the mirror with Jake behind her, lifted her heavy hair, and bent her head forward. He carefully clasped the pendant around her neck then planted a tender kiss on her nape. She released her hair to swing over her shoulders and down her back.

Their eyes met in the mirror. The desire that sparked from his set her body on fire. She leaned against his broad chest.

He wrapped one arm around her waist and pulled her closer. With his free hand, he touched the pendant, rubbing the stone. "This is pretty, but you deserve emeralds and diamonds."

"Emeralds?"

"To match your eyes." Slowly, deliberately, he dragged his fingers down her chest to the neckline of her dress. He caressed the swell of her breasts, spilling out from her lacy push-up bra. When he slipped a hand inside to massage one breast, her nipples tightened and she groaned softly.

She watched in the mirror as he fondled her. Her lips were parted and her eyes were passion-glazed. She looked like the star of her own sexual fantasy. But this was no fantasy. This was so much better.

"I can't wait to get you out of these clothes and make you mine again," he whispered.

"I can't either," she said in a husky voice.

He pulled away and turned her to face him. "We'd better get down there now because if we stay here one minute longer, we won't show up for the party."

With a smile, Graceann grabbed the green wrap from the bed. Jake slipped it over her shoulders, kissing each shoulder before covering it with the silk.

Holding hands, they left the room and walked down the stairs just as Kate and her boyfriend arrived. Kate's eyes slid from surprise to suspicion as she watched Graceann and Jake descend the stairs.

When they reached the bottom, the women hugged. Graceann turned to Kate's date and smiled. "Happy New Year, Brian."

He gave her a quick hug. "Happy New Year to you, too."

Graceann grabbed Jake's hand and drew him forward. "Jake, you know Kate. This is her friend Brian."

Kate hugged Jake. "Nice to see you again."

"You, too," he said.

As the men shook hands, they seemed to size each other up. Graceann hid her grin. Men were no different from women, checking out the competition. Jake had nothing to worry about. No other man could compare to him.

"Let's get this party started." Kate turned to Brian. "Would you mind getting me a glass of white wine?"

"Sure, sweetheart."

Jake nodded toward Graceann. "Do you want some wine, too?"

"Thank you. White is fine."

"The bar is this way," Jake said to Brian.

As the men headed toward the great room, Kate grabbed Graceann's arm and pulled her into the living room, away from the other arriving guests.

The string quartet Graceann's mother hired began to tune their instruments in a corner of the room.

Kate gave them an annoyed look and motioned to Graceann to follow her into the corner farthest away from the music.

"What?" Graceann asked once they were huddled together.

"Don't play innocent. What is going on between you and The Falcon?"

Graceann brushed hair back from her face, then

met her friend's gaze. "It's Jake, and nothing's going on. We're still pretending to be engaged."

Kate put her hand on her hip and shot Graceann a look filled with disbelief. "If that's acting, I'll buy you each a ticket to Hollywood. My God, woman, you're in love with the guy. How the heck did that happen?"

Graceann took a step back. "I'm not in love with him. In lust maybe, but that's all it is."

"Girlfriend, you are in denial. You've fallen in love with The Falcon."

"No, I haven't."

Kate's eyes grew wider. "Oh. My. God. You've slept with him!" She moved closer and looked around. No one else had come into the room. In a conspiratorial whisper, she asked, "What's he like?"

Graceann bristled. "I never kiss and tell."

"Ah-ha! You admit you slept with him."

"I admit nothing."

Kate's expression turned serious and she put a hand on Graceann's arm. "What do you know about him? He looks like the same Falcon to me. You're risking your heart again. What happens when Jake rides out of town?"

"I won't get hurt." The lie stuck in her chest. She'd fallen hard for Jake. When they parted he'd take a huge chunk of her heart with him.

"What kind of work does he do?" Kate asked. "Where does he live?"

"I don't know."

Kate dug her fingers into Graceann's arm, making Graceann wince. "Didn't you learn anything from Michael? I'm sorry I talked you into hiring him to be your fake fiancé. I have a feeling this won't end well. Please be careful."

"I can take care of myself." Despite her words, anxiety took a firm hold in Graceann's heart. Kate had voiced the doubts Graceann had been ignoring.

Her thoughts were interrupted as guests, holding plates of food and goblets of wine, drifted into the room. Jake and Brian came back, each holding two glasses. Jake had a glass of wine for her and a club soda with a twist of lime for himself. When he handed Graceann her drink, his fingers lingered over hers.

"Happy New Year, baby," he said, his voice a low rasp.

By ten-thirty the party was in full swing. Jake stood in the great room sipping on his club soda, taking a welcome respite from all the mingling and mixing. Smiling at the carefree picture Graceann and Lorrie presented as they talked and laughed across the room with some of their friends, he inhaled the aroma of pinecones and apple pie that wafted throughout the house. After this holiday, those scents would always bring bittersweet thoughts of love and family, two things that might always be missing from his life. When the stink of gin drifted to him from the bar, his stomach clenched with painful memories of Christmases in the Falco household. He moved to a spot farther away from the bar and drank deeply of his club soda, as if he could wash away the memories that never left him.

He'd made polite conversation with many of the party guests. Some of them had looked at him in puzzlement, as if they might know him. He wondered if they recognized him from the years he'd lived there or if they'd heard of him through his films. He dismissed that last thought. Only the most dedicated film buffs knew his work. He smiled. If things went the way he hoped, that might all be about to change.

Although he was good at mingling, he'd never enjoyed forced gaiety. The New Year's joy here tonight seemed genuine. The holiday parties he'd attended the last few years were glitzy events in over-decorated houses, where most of the guests attended to see and be seen. They were cold affairs lacking the old-fashioned good cheer he'd found with Graceann's family and friends.

His heart seemed to stick in his throat as he watched Graceann laugh at something Lorrie said. Graceann was hot, but more importantly, she possessed a refreshing charm he didn't think existed in many females these days. She looked happy, had looked that way all evening. He liked to think he'd put that smile on her face. Their lovemaking had been special, something he would always treasure.

Happiness. The word came out of nowhere and burst through him like New Year's fireworks. He looked at the others gathered in small groups in the room. People enjoying each other's company. Like the sun breaking through dark clouds, he saw it all clearly now. This was what normal people did. They liked each other, were glad to be together.

Accustomed to being around dealmakers and dating women who wanted him for his connections, he'd forgotten how regular people acted. Even Graceann's mother, despite driving everyone crazy with the preparations, only wanted her guests to enjoy themselves.

It had been too long since anything in his life seemed real. He'd gotten so cynical.

Graceann belonged in this world with these decent people who had deep roots. The demands of his work dictated he move around, and he had invested too much sweat equity to stop. A thought edged into his mind, stilling him. Maybe if he had a woman like Graceann waiting for him, he'd have a reason to stay in one place.

"If it isn't Jake Falco." The slurred voice at Jake's elbow jerked him from his melancholy thoughts.

Jake turned his head to meet the cloudy gray eyes of Chad Wentworth, star quarterback when Jake was in school. He'd noticed Chad earlier but had avoided him. Chad and his fellow jocks had done all they could to make life hell for Jake and his friends.

Looking at the overweight, fleshy-faced Wentworth, Jake felt nothing. Before this holiday with Graceann, he might have sneered at Wentworth, or let his anger about his treatment at the guy's hands take hold.

"Wentworth," Jake said. "What are you up to nowadays? Still playing football?"

The guy guzzled some of the beer from the bottle he held, then released a bitter laugh. "Do I look like I play football?" He patted his protruding belly. "I run my dad's hardware store here in town. I haven't seen you since graduation. Where have you been?"

"Los Angeles."

"Doing what?" Wentworth stumbled slightly and Jake reached out to steady him.

Resisting the urge to wrinkle his nose at the overwhelming stench of beer emanating from Wentworth, Jake said, "I'm doing odd jobs out in L.A. Mostly house painting." He fought back the temptation to gloat a little. He hated to lie, but he'd be damned if he'd tell this jerk the truth that Graceann and her family didn't yet know.

"Not made much of yourself, I see," Wentworth said in a smug voice.

Jake shrugged. Let the guy believe what he wanted. Jake owed him nothing.

An overweight, heavily made-up woman, vaguely familiar, walked up to them. She took the beer bottle out of Wentworth's hand and set it on a nearby tray for empty glasses. "You've had enough. We need to leave."

"This here's the little wife," Wentworth said to Jake. "You remember Tiffany, don't you?"

She looked at Jake then, and recognition hit him like a bullet between the eyes. "Tiffany Johnson," he said. She'd been head cheerleader, the sexiest, most popular girl in school, and he'd wanted her. She'd seduced him one memorable night as they sat in her Mustang. Then she'd laughed about it with her friends, mocking Jake. The hurt had stayed with him for years.

"Jake Falco?" She scanned him with brown eyes he used to think beautiful. "You're looking good. Real good."

"Thanks." He signaled the bartender for another club soda. He wished Wentworth and his wife would leave.

The three of them stood in awkward silence for a moment. Then Tiffany took her husband's arm and pulled him away. "Nice seeing you again, Jake." They marched out.

Jake sighed with relief. To think as a kid he'd wasted anger and hurt on those two.

He sensed someone's stare and raised his gaze to find Graceann smiling at him from across the room.

With a graceful sway of hips, she headed his way. Her smile and her sweetness knocked down the last bit of wall protecting his heart. Later, he'd figure out how to reconstruct the barrier he'd so painstakingly built since childhood.

Tonight belonged to Graceann.

Finally, midnight approached. Graceann stood in the great room with most of the other guests. They'd crowded into the room ready to watch the ball descend on Times Square signaling the New Year.

Holding a flute of champagne, she nervously looked around for Jake. He'd had a phone call twenty minutes ago and disappeared. More mystery from him. The anxiety that had balled in her chest when she'd talked to Kate earlier returned full force as she wondered what secrets he kept.

She looked at the time on the TV screen. Eleven fifty-six. She wanted a New Year's kiss from Jake, but that wouldn't happen if he didn't get back soon. They hadn't much more time together.

This year's Christmas celebrations would be etched on her mind forever because of Jake. He'd made this whole holiday new, fresh, and exciting. She saw everything through his eyes—the special love her family felt for each other, the way they unselfishly cared about each other. She even saw more clearly why her parents wanted her to find a good man, a man to spend her life with. They wanted her to have what they'd found.

She would never have believed Jake could be a family man, but he'd shown her a softer side of him she suspected he kept hidden from most others. They would split up in a few days to go their separate ways. A part of her heart broke at the thought. She wanted to beg him to stay with her. She couldn't. They had a business agreement. That's all it was. The spirit of the holiday had gotten to her. Once she was back in New York, this whole interlude with Jake would be another pleasant memory.

She almost believed it.

She felt someone move to stand behind her. Inhaling Jake's unique scent of soap and spice, she smiled and turned around. Her heart did a little flip.

He'd loosened his tie, taken off his jacket and rolled up his sleeves. Every cell in her body went on alert.

He slipped his arm around her waist and drew her close. "I missed you," he whispered.

She noticed her sister andLorrie some of the other guests watching them. Lorrie gave her a knowing smile and held up her champagne flute in salute. Graceann snuggled closer to Jake and returned her sister's smile.

"Everything okay?" Graceann asked.

"Couldn't be better." He gave her a wide grin.

That phone call seemed to have lightened his

mood, but hers dropped several notches. He still wasn't sharing anything in his life beyond their fake relationship, reinforcing that after he left, he'd be gone for good.

She glanced away as the crowd around them started chanting. "Ten. Nine. Eight. Seven. Six. Five. Four. Three. Two. One. *Happy New Year!*"

Jake turned her around to face him. He took the champagne flute from her and set it on a nearby table. Then he pulled her into his arms. "Happy New Year, sweetheart."

"Happy New Year, Jake."

He kissed her hard and deep with an urgency that matched her hunger for him and made her forget her fears of a minute ago. Her body stirred in response.

"Hey, you two, break it up." Lorrie's laughing voice came from behind Graceann. "Others want to wish you Happy New Year, too."

A hot flush spread up Graceann's neck and she reluctantly pulled away from Jake. Then everyone kissed and hugged them, intruding on their little bubble.

Jake didn't think the guests would ever leave. He wanted to be alone with Graceann, wanted to hold her, to make love to her. He needed her.

That phone call earlier had brought the news

he'd hoped for. Finally, he had something he felt comfortable sharing with her, and he would. He never thought he'd want to share his life with a woman.

Until Graceann.

At three o'clock in the morning, the last of the guests left. Graceann's grandmother had gone to bed hours ago. Graceann's mother began to clear away dirty plates until her husband stopped her. "We're all tired. Let's get to bed. The caterers will be back later today to clean up."

"Yeah, Mom, let it go," Lorrie said.

As the others headed up the stairs, Lorrie looked back at Graceann and Jake standing in the foyer. "You two coming up?"

"In a little while," Graceann said.

When the others disappeared upstairs, Jake gathered Graceann into his arms. "I never thought we'd be alone."

She wound her arms around his neck. "I didn't either. I want you, Jake. Now."

Her words and the softness in her eyes were almost his undoing. He would leave her soon.

He couldn't.

Maybe he didn't have to. That phone call changed everything.

Feeling more hopeful than he had in a long time, he cupped her face between his hands. "I want to give you a proper New Year's celebration and make slow love to you all night. We'll make our own fireworks."

She stood on tiptoe and kissed him. "That's what I want, too."

Chapter Fourteen

GRACEANN TOOK JAKE'S HAND as they ran up the stairs. When he saw the deserted hallway, he breathed a sigh of relief. Outside Graceann's room, he gripped her shoulders and turned her to face him. "I'm coming in."

"I know."

They slipped through her door and Jake closed it with his foot. He backed her up against the wall and braced his hands above her head. She licked her lips and raised her gaze to his. Desire and longing sparked from her eyes. She'd never looked more beautiful and desirable. At that moment he wanted nothing more than to make love to her, to hold her close forever, to cherish her, to protect her.

He slid his hand beneath the silky mass of her

hair and cupped the back of her head, then kissed her with a hunger only she could ease. She pressed close and kissed him back with an urgency that filled him with masculine pride and wrapped around his heart. He was so hard he thought his cock would burst through the zipper of his pants. Hell, he'd been hard most of the night with wanting her.

But it was more.

He needed her.

She gasped when he slipped her dress off her shoulders and massaged her breasts through the lace covering them. Still kissing her, he reached behind her to unclasp her bra, freeing her breasts. Her incredible breasts.

Her hands slid up his chest to wind around his neck, and she loosened the cord holding his hair, freeing it to fall around his shoulders. With a sigh, she tunneled her fingers through it.

He left her full, soft lips to rain kisses down the smooth column of her throat. Clutching his shoulders, she threw back her head. That she gave herself so freely to him knocked down more of the barriers around his heart. He wanted to absorb her into his very soul, to love her so completely she'd never want another man.

He bent to suckle one puckered nipple then the other. He caressed her breasts again, pressing them together and flicking his tongue along her deep cleavage.

He picked her up and felt her body tremble as he carried her to the bed, then deposited her onto the white comforter. With her dress bunched around her waist and her perfect breasts bared, she was a fiery temptress who'd captured his heart so completely he knew a life without her would be empty. Only Graceann could make him whole.

She gave him a sultry look from lowered lashes, and like a man possessed, all thoughts fled except his fierce need to have her. He stripped off his clothes, throwing them aside, then joined her on the bed.

He made quick work of her shoes, dress, and thong. When he bent his head to suckle the hard peak of one full, heavy breast, she rubbed herself against him. He kept up his erotic assault, kissing and massaging her sensitive breasts. Intoxicated by her willing body, he felt ready to explode. Through sheer force of will he controlled himself. All he cared about now was her pleasure. Moaning deeply, she fisted her hand in his hair, and he knew she was on the brink. Her trust, her complete surrender to him, filled him with a yearning so strong it frightened him. There was no going back. He'd always belong to her. Crying out his name, she stiffened, then fell apart in shuddering waves.

He held her quivering body until she stilled. "Jake," she said again on a hoarse whisper.

Her mixture of strength and vulnerability bound him to her like ropes of velvet holding him a willing prisoner. He gladly relinquished his body and soul. The softness and trust in her gaze touched his core, healing some of the hurt and pain he'd hidden for so long.

"Graceann." He touched her face in wonder that this slip of a woman could so entrance him and make him want her in a way that was in turn painful and awesome. He'd lived so long afraid to love. Her faith in him was rapidly breaking down the last of the wall he'd erected around his heart.

Succumbing to her spell and his powerful need, he slowly kissed his way down her body, nipping and licking her smooth, hot skin. She arched her hips in frank invitation. When he kissed her trimmed thatch of dark hair, she keened, low and deep.

He slipped his fingers into her wetness. She was so ready for him. He stroked the sensitive nub between her legs and spread her folds. When he dipped his tongue inside her sultry heat she wound her fingers into his hair and opened wider.

He drove his tongue deep, tasting her essence. She whispered his name on a tortured breath. Delighting in taking her higher and higher, he sucked and kissed. His need for her built, his loins tightened, and he drove harder and deeper, tasting her, loving her. Screaming her pleasure, she pulled on his hair as she exploded around him.

Making his way back up her body, he kissed her breasts, her throat, her sweet, inviting lips. She opened to him, her ravenous tongue dueling with his, her pliant body eager for him. He couldn't wait any longer. He grabbed a condom from the pocket of his pants and pulled it over his cock.

Pressing her into the mattress, he settled himself over her and drove into her. This was where he belonged, with her. He thrust hard and deep. She wrapped her legs around his hips and met his every stroke as he drove his hips against hers, submerged in her heat, his body on fire, every nerve in him aching for her love.

He kissed her feverishly, urgently as he pounded into her. Her fingers dug into his back and she arched her hips to take in more of him. Making guttural sounds, she began to tremble and raked her fingernails into his skin. Her body shook as her orgasm built. She grew still, then shuddered, crying out her pleasure.

Before she had a chance to recover, he rolled over, taking her with him, his cock still sheathed in her softness. Her breathing ragged, her eyes green as rich, dark emeralds, she straddled him.

Her long, thick hair swung around her face and over her breasts. She rode him hard and fast, her face tight with need. He filled his hands with her breasts and arched to meet her. She threw back her head, and with one long, drawn-out shudder, she climaxed again.

Only then did he allow himself the release he so desperately needed. He gripped her waist with his hands and let his orgasm roll over him in wild waves. He bit his lip, suppressing his cry. Finally, he lay still. Graceann collapsed on top of him.

He stroked her sweat-sheened back as she buried her face in his neck. After long minutes, she pulled away to look down at him.

"Wow!"

He laughed and pressed her against him again. Jake felt content, satisfied. He'd come home.

When their breathing returned to normal, Graceann rolled off him. Facing each other, inches apart, he smoothed hair back from her face and twirled strands of the silky softness between his fingers. "Liked that, did you?"

"The best start ever to a new year," she said with a soft laugh. "Do you think anyone heard us?"

"Probably."

"Oh, God."

He chuckled. "Don't worry. We're supposed to be engaged."

Her features tensed. "Jake, it's almost over."

He placed a finger over her lips. "Don't talk about it. We have today."

Her throat worked as she swallowed. "We have to talk about it. We leave tomorrow. You said you don't want my money. Why did you take the job if you didn't want the money?"

His chest tightened and he twisted onto his back. With effort, he pulled his heart into the locked box where he'd kept it all these years, hiding it away from the foolish thoughts he'd had in the throes of passion. He'd never known real love, wasn't sure what it felt like. He didn't know if he was capable of giving Graceann the kind of love she needed and deserved.

"I used to see you in school," he finally said. "I would look at you, at how sweet, innocent, and kind you were, and I wondered what it would be like to be part of your life. When you asked me to help you with this charade, I took it as my chance to see how the other side lives."

"Oh, Jake." She moved closer, and propping herself on one elbow, stroked a finger down his arm. Every nerve in his body responded. He wanted to claim her again, to never leave her.

"What if I want to keep seeing you?" she asked, a hesitant note in her voice.

He turned to face her. "We've had a great time, Graceann, but reality looks a lot different than these past nine days. You might not want me when you go back to the real world."

"I'll want you, Jake. I'll always want you."

The hurt in her eyes aimed straight for his heart. Oh, hell, he was tired of being noble. Yes, she deserved the best of everything, but he couldn't let her go. Hope rushed through him. Maybe he was selling himself short, and her, too. Things were looking up for him. His career was on an upward spiral. He had a lot to be proud of, a lot to offer her.

The tension and fear that were always present began to squeeze out his hope, but he fought it back. For Graceann, he'd let love into his heart.

She drew circles on his chest with her finger. "Where will you go now?"

"Home."

"Where's home?"

"My base is Los Angeles, but I'm seldom there." He grabbed her hand to stop her from drawing the lazy circles. "If you keep doing that, I won't be able to think, let alone talk, and we need to talk."

Her eyes, large and trusting, looked deeply into his. "We do need to talk."

He rubbed his thumb along her cheekbone. "Graceann, this Christmas with your family has been the best I've ever spent," he began. "I'll always be grateful to you for giving me that gift."

"Thank you for saying that." Her eyes glistened. With tears? "Was it hard growing up the way you did, with both parents alcoholics? Did they always drink?"

Startled by her abrupt change of subject, he rolled onto his back again. "My childhood was like scenes from a dark and dreary Swedish film. My dad drank from as long back as I can remember. My mom didn't at first. I have some good memories of her caring for me, watching out for me. I think she began drinking to keep Dad company. I believe she really loved him and she felt if she drank along with him, she'd show her love."

"Codependency. That's sad and kind of sick."

"Yeah, it is. That's what love does to people."

"No, it doesn't, not to most. Is that why you're afraid to love?"

He sucked in an unsteady breath. "I'm not afraid. I'm realistic."

"You've never had a real Christmas?"

"Not since I was very little."

"Jake, I'm so sorry."

He turned and took her into his arms. "I don't want your pity."

"What do you want?"

"You."

They drew out their lovemaking, taking each other tenderly, as if they both knew it might be their last time together. He worshipped her body, imprinting every curve and hollow, every sigh and smile, onto his mind.

Spent, they lay in each other's arms. Finally, Jake took a deep breath and pulled free. He rolled onto his back and stared at the ceiling. The softness of dawn filtered into the room. The dawn of a new day. Of a new year. And new resolutions. "Graceann, you need to know the truth about me. I'm a filmmaker and a screenwriter with a fair amount of success."

When she didn't react, he looked down at her. She was fast asleep. He smiled and gathered her to him. "Happy New Year, love."

He would tell her later, as soon as she woke.

They were awakened by a loud knocking at the bedroom door. Jolted upright, Jake looked at the clock. Nine. His head throbbed. They'd only gotten to sleep a few hours ago.

Next to him, Graceann shot up and gave him a questioning look. Another more insistent knock had her out of bed. She threw on her robe and cautiously opened the door a crack to peer out.

"Mom!"

Shit. Jake pulled the covers up to his chin.

"I know Jake's with you," her mother said. "Your father and I want to see both of you, now, in your father's office."

"What's going on?" Graceann asked.

"Come down please and we'll talk."

Graceann closed the door and faced Jake. "Daddy never calls a meeting in his office unless it's something very serious."

Chapter Fifteen

JAKE AND GRACEANN dressed hurriedly. She pulled on yoga pants and a long-sleeved top. Jake slipped on his pants and shirt and hurried off to his room to change. Confused thoughts jumbled through Graceann's head as they met up together in the hallway, Jake now wearing jeans and a sweater, then ran down the stairs to her father's office. Her parents thought she and Jake were engaged, so she doubted they were upset because they'd slept together. It had to be something else, something very bad.

"I hope it's not Grandmom again," Graceann huffed, slightly out of breath.

When they got to the office door, Jake took her hand. "Whatever it is, I'm with you."

Graceann managed a smile. With Jake by her side she could face whatever her parents sent her way.

Feeling much stronger, she held his hand as they walked in, closing the door behind them. Her dad was standing in front of his massive walnut desk, his features tense. Her mother stood by the window, nervously rubbing her hands together.

"What is it, Daddy?" Graceann released Jake's hand and crossed her arms over her midriff to hide her trembling.

Her father ignored her and directed an anger-filled gaze at Jake. "You came into our home, accepted our hospitality, and all along you were using us. How were you going to portray us in the movie? As country bumpkins fooled by the big shot Hollywood producer?"

Jake stepped back as if punched. "It wasn't like that. I can explain."

Frowning, Graceann looked from Jake to her father. "What are you talking about, Daddy?"

Her father leaned against the desk, as if his legs could no longer support him, and grasped the edges with white-knuckled hands. "Max Stewart stopped by last night for a short while on his way to another event."

"Max Stewart?" Graceann said.

"Editor of the *Spirit Lake Times*."

"What does that have to do with us?" she asked.

"Max heard about your engagement. He told me one of his reporters would call me this morning for a comment. They plan to run a story in tomorrow's paper. I assumed they were going to do a fluff piece. I just hung up with the reporter. They're not writing a segment for the society page, but for the front page."

Beside her, she felt Jake stiffen.

"I don't understand," she said.

"What don't you understand?" Her father stepped away from the desk. "You don't understand why we'd be upset that you lied to us about your fiancé?"

Her mother left the window and came to stand next to her husband. "Graceann, how could you keep something like this from us?"

"How did the newspaper editor know about Jake?" Only she, Kate, and Jake knew. And why would the newspaper care that she'd hired a fake fiancé? She was going to be sick. This wasn't going the way she'd planned at all.

"How did the newspaper get hold of the story?" Jake asked.

Her father looked at Jake. "Your producer friends hung around town for awhile and they like to talk."

"Producer friends?" Graceann turned to Jake, but he ignored her, his attention on her father.

"What did the reporter say?" Jake asked in a tight voice.

"I think you know," her father answered. "He wanted a comment on how I felt about my daughter marrying Jake Falco, Hollywood screenwriter, producer, and actor who was in town scouting locations for his latest film, a scathing depiction of Spirit Lake and its citizens."

"It's not what it seems," Jake said.

Lightheaded and nauseous, Graceann grabbed Jake's arm, forcing him to meet her gaze. "What's he talking about?" Her voice came out thin and shaking.

"I planned to tell you, Graceann," he said. "They had no right to leak that. We haven't signed the contract yet. What they said about the movie is bogus. Yes, I'm here to scout locations but the movie won't show Spirit Lake in a bad light. Not anymore. You've got to believe me."

"Believe you? You're a screenwriter, a producer? An actor, for God's sake. You're making a movie here? And you never bothered to tell me?" Anger slammed into her and she fought a new wave of nausea.

"You didn't know about this?" her father asked.

Graceann pulled air through her lungs and shifted her attention to her parents. "No, Daddy, I didn't."

"You thought your fiancé repaired motorcycles?" her mom asked in an incredulous voice.

Guilt mixed with Graceann's anger. "I knew he didn't fix motorcycles. I wasn't sure what he did."

"You don't know what type work your fiancé does?" her mom echoed.

Her dad rubbed a hand over his forehead and sat on the edge of the desk, his face pale. "One of you explain what the hell is going on."

"We need to tell them everything." Jake reached out to grab one of Graceann's hands.

She jerked away. "Don't touch me." The shock that flashed across his face cut into her heart. She'd hurt him, but he'd lied to her, or rather he'd kept the truth about himself from her. She'd lied to her family.

Karma was a bitch.

She twisted her ring, her faux engagement ring, around her finger, and focused on the opposite wall. Isabella's framed drawings in clashing crayon colors were hung there. The wildly mixed colors in the drawings matched her thoughts—mixed-up, chaotic, confused. She turned her gaze to her parents' bewildered ones. "Jake's not my fiancé. I—I hired him to play the part."

Her mother gasped and put her hand to her mouth. Her father sat straighter, his body rigid. If looks could wound, she'd be maimed now, along with Jake.

"Why. Would. You. Do. That?" her father said between gritted teeth.

Soft footsteps sounded outside, then a light knock on the door. Before anyone could respond,

Grandmom came into the room and stopped, her gaze shifting among the others.

"Something wrong? I heard raised voices," Grandmom said.

"Jake is not Graceann's fiancé," her mother said. "She lied to us. And that's not the only lie."

Head shaking, Grandmom turned to Graceann. "I told you, child, that you needed to tell your parents the truth."

"You knew, Mom, and you didn't say anything?" Graceann's father's voice rose several octaves as he faced his mother.

"Settle down, Mark, and let the girl talk." Her grandmother sank into a leather chair next to the desk and looked expectantly at Graceann.

Her parents turned anxious looks Graceann's way, too. "What possessed you to hire a fiancé?" her father asked.

Graceann continued to twist the ring around her finger. It dug into her flesh but she didn't care. She welcomed the pain. Physical pain was preferable to this gut-wrenching audience with her parents. "I thought if I had a fiancé, Mom would quit trying to fix me up with some guy."

Her mom bristled. "You're blaming me?"

"No, Mom, no. Of course not." God, she was handling this badly. She felt like a six-year-old getting a scolding. But she wasn't a child. She was a grown woman and she'd take responsibility for her actions. Beside her, Jake stood unmoving, only his ragged breathing a testimony to his raw emotions.

"I only want you to meet a nice man and settle down," her mother said.

"I know, but I can find my own guys." Graceann was surprised at the calmness in her voice. "Besides I don't want to get married, at least not for awhile. I only want you to let me live my life and not try to arrange it for me."

"We're not trying to arrange your life," her dad said. "This is the craziest thing you've ever done. How long were you planning to keep up this false engagement?"

"After the holidays, I planned to tell you Jake and I broke up, that I didn't love him and it was my decision. I figured if you thought I was finally over Michael and in control of my life, you'd let me live it my own way."

"Graceann, how could you fool us like this?" Tears shone in her mother's eyes, twisting the knife of guilt deeper into Graceann.

"I'm sorry. I didn't mean to hurt you."

"But you *have* hurt us and disappointed us." Her father turned his angry gaze to Jake. "Did you think you'd get more fodder for your movie by living with us, observing us, mocking us?"

"My movie had nothing to do with my going along with Graceann's, uh—charade," Jake said in a harsh voice. "I knew Graceann from school. I wanted to help her."

Notching her chin up, Graceann looked at Jake. "Were you making fun of us all? What role would I play in your little movie?"

Hurt flashed across his features. But he wasn't the man she'd thought he was. It had happened to her again. Kate was right. She'd learned nothing from the debacle with Michael.

"We've gotten close these last few days," Jake said, his voice low. "Have I acted in any way like I'm making fun of you, or using you?"

"No, but you're an actor."

He stepped closer. She dropped her hands to her sides, but didn't move away.

"I never acted with you, Graceann. Not once. When I wrote the script, a lot of my bitterness toward this town and its treatment of me and my family came out. I hadn't intended that to happen, but it did. My original pitch was that the movie would be *Footloose* meets *Shaun of the Dead*. That's no longer the case. The revised version will show Spirit Lake as a decent place with good people."

"I have a hard time believing that," Graceann said.

"I don't know what to believe," her mother said.

Her father cleared his throat. The others looked at him. "Let me get this straight. You hired this man you barely know to come into our house?"

Graceann blinked back tears. "I did know Jake, sort of."

Her father waved a hand in dismissal at Jake. "I think you'd better leave, young man."

"I'll leave, sir." Jake nodded to her grandmother. "I'm sorry, Mrs. Palmer." He switched his gaze to her parents. "Mr. and Mrs. Palmer, I meant no ill-will toward any of you. You treated me like a member of the family and I'll always be grateful." Without looking at Graceann, he strode out of the room.

"I can't fathom you had the audacity to bring a stranger into our home, Graceann," her father said. "I never knew you to be the reckless type."

Grandmom stood. "I think we all need to take a little time to breathe."

"I'm going to talk to Jake." Graceann slipped out of the room. The beginnings of a throbbing headache pounded her, but she needed answers—now.

She found him in his room packing. "Jake," she said from the doorway.

He turned to her with stormy blue eyes. "Come to make sure I'm not stealing the silver?"

She walked closer. "You wouldn't do that."

"Tell that to your parents. I saw the looks they gave me. The fine, upstanding people of Spirit Lake used to look at my family that way. That judgment of me based on my parents is why I couldn't wait to put this town behind me."

186

"You told me you held no hard feelings about this town. You lied. You do want revenge. You wrote a movie that will give you that."

He threw the shirt he held onto the bed and met her eyes. "I thought I learned a long time ago not to waste my energy on revenge. Apparently I was wrong. When I wrote the original script, my pent-up anger and bitterness came out, and it did show this town in a bad way. Now that I've gotten to know you and your family, I recognize the goodness of the people here, their kindness."

"Spare me."

His features tightened. Hurt shadowed his eyes. "Think what you will. I'm revising the script. It's now *Twilight* meets *Shaun of the Dead,* a zombie teen love story." He smoothed a hand over his hair. "When I pitched it the other day to my partner and the backers, I was afraid they'd reject the new story arc. That phone call last night was my partner telling me we had the backing. This is the break we've been waiting for."

When she remained silent, he went back to tossing clothes into his duffel.

She fought tears. She was happy for his success, but he'd not been honest with her. He hadn't trusted her. How could she have been so wrong about him? "Why didn't you tell me what you do? A screenwriter and producer? That's something to be proud of. You know how I feel about men who lie, about men who have hidden lives."

He didn't look at her, but continued packing. "I didn't lie to you. I just didn't tell you everything."

"Omitting is lying."

He turned then and walked slowly toward her. When he reached her, he cupped her shoulders, his gaze intense. She knew she should step back from him, but she didn't want to. She wanted this whole nightmare to go away.

"If you knew the truth, would it have made a difference?" he asked. "Would you have treated me differently?"

"Yes. No. I don't know what you mean."

Disappointment washed over his features and he released her. "I guess you don't."

She scrubbed a hand over her face. "Why did you agree to my fake fiancé scheme?"

He leaned against the dresser with his arms folded across his chest. His relaxed stance belied the tension evident in every taut line of his body. "I was going to tell you the truth, even brag a little, that first day in the diner, but then you offered me money, and I figured you thought I was a loser, like most everyone else in this town."

"I never thought of you as a loser."

"Didn't you? You had a schoolgirl vision of me, maybe even a crush. I'm not that pseudo bad-boy. I never was. I didn't do half the things I was accused of." His gaze held hers. He stepped toward her. "Admit you liked the excitement of being with The Falcon."

Truth be told, at first she had pegged him as someone who'd never pulled up from his poor beginnings. And yes, she'd always found his bad-boy persona exciting.

Her legs felt wobbly and she sat on the edge of the bed. "The newspaper reporter said you're an actor, too. When we made love, was that acting? Did you mean all those things you said, all you did?"

His features softened and he came to sit beside her. Touching her chin with his fingers, he waited until she looked at him. "I meant every word, every kiss. Making love to you was the most real thing I've ever done."

She pulled free of his scorching touch. Her instincts told her Jake Falco was a decent and caring person, that she'd gotten to know the real man. But she wasn't a good judge of men. "You haven't answered my question. Why did you agree to go along with my plan, especially if you didn't need the money?"

He drew a deep breath and glanced away. "I used to see your family around town. I thought you couldn't be real, that families weren't kind and considerate toward each other. I wanted to prove to myself deep down that you were no different from my family. But I've learned your family is real and loving and good. Even now, with your parents angry at you, it's obvious they love you very much."

When he turned back to her, she read unhappiness in his eyes, but something else, something that made her pulse jump.

"And I wanted to know the woman you've become," he said. "No matter what's happened, how much of a mess we've made of things, I'll never regret getting to know you, Graceann."

Before she knew what was happening, he brushed his lips over hers, sweetly and gently, then pulled away. "I'll always treasure the time we spent together, making love with you, laughing with you."

She pressed a hand to her unsettled stomach. "You could have gotten to know me and my family and still told me the truth about what you do."

"Yeah, I could have. But I can be stubborn. I wanted you to accept me, the real me, Jake Falco, the guy I am, the guy I've always been, someone from a small town who's worked hard and paid his dues. I wanted you to want me, not some hot-shot Hollywood type. And maybe I wanted to see how a normal family spends Christmas."

"How did you end up in Hollywood?" she asked.

He shrugged. "I took all the money I'd saved from my after-school job, jumped on that old, restored motorcycle and started driving west. I slept in shelters in the cities and outdoors in the rural areas. Got to L.A., found a hovel of an apartment, did whatever work came my way—painting houses, waiting tables. And I wrote every spare minute. Through my restaurant job, I made good contacts in the industry and got a few acting gigs in low-budget indies. A producer I met liked one of my screenplays and bought it. And that's my story."

"You make it sound so easy."

His lips tilted in a wry smile. "It took me eight years to become an overnight success, but I was lucky."

"And talented."

"That, too, I guess." He rose from the bed and finished filling his duffel, then zipped it closed with a finality that stung her heart. He was leaving and she'd never see him again. He hadn't trusted her. He'd withheld the truth. He had a hidden life, like Michael. She couldn't accept that.

Fluffy ran into the room and began barking at Jake. With a wry smile, he said, "I won't miss that dog."

"Fluffy, get out of here," she said. To her surprise, the dog obeyed and trotted out of the room. She wanted to ask Jake if he'd miss her, but she couldn't.

"I called a car," he said. "It should be here any minute."

She stood, rubbing her arms. "Where will you go?"

"To my condo in Bremer first, then Los Angeles. I

have reservations on a flight out tomorrow morning."

"You have a condo in the next town?" A new rush of anger hit her. "Another *secret*."

"I bought it a month ago so I'd have a place to stay while shooting the movie." He picked up his duffel and garment bag, then dropped them on the floor.

He was by her side in an instant. Pulling her against him, he kissed her hard, almost brutally. She stiffened, resisting him, then melted and returned his kiss. His lips softened and he moaned low in his throat. She opened to him, wanting to recapture the oneness they'd had when they'd made love.

He ended the kiss and held her at arm's length, his breathing ragged. "Come with me."

"To California?"

He nodded. "Let's see where this thing between us is going. I can afford to take care of you."

Every nerve in her body screamed for her to go with him, but pride had her backing away. Hands clenched at her sides, she all but hissed. "*See* where 'this thing between us is going'? You can *afford* me? I have a life here and I can take care of myself. I've been doing it for awhile now."

"Graceann—"

She looked him right in the eye. Enough was enough. "It's best you leave."

Graceann lay face down on her bed. She'd cried

until she had no more tears left. She'd hurt her family with her lies, maybe even hurt Jake. He'd hurt her. He hadn't trusted her enough to tell her the truth. Now he was gone.

Deep in her heart she believed he couldn't have been acting when they made love. She'd seen the passion and tenderness in his eyes, felt it in his kisses and his touch. Their lovemaking had been magical. He'd wanted her to want the real him. He had to care for her, at least a little. But he had a funny way of showing it, with his talk about "this thing between us." For her it was a lot more than a "thing."

Jake was no better than Michael, hiding the truth. No, Jake wasn't anything like Michael. Michael had never been tender. His passion had been polished, that of a man more interested in impressing a woman than in making her feel loved. He was the one who'd been playing a part throughout their affair, not Jake. And when she'd confronted Michael with the truth, he'd shown no remorse, and couldn't figure out why she wouldn't want to be with him, why she didn't care about his money and influence. Jake was no Michael.

Rolling over, she stared at the ceiling. This whole ordeal had taught her a hard lesson. The adage, "Honesty is the best policy," sprang to mind.

Brushing hair away from her face, she sat up. Her cell phone lay on the nightstand. She grabbed it and clicked on her photos, wanting to see Jake's face.

Slowly, fighting tears, she scanned through the pictures she'd taken during the holiday. There they were—she and Jake and Isabella standing proudly by the snowman. She and Jake in front of the Christmas tree in the foyer, in the kitchen preparing Christmas dinner, with Kate and Brian at the party. In each picture Jake was smiling. He looked happy. That wasn't acting, she was sure of it. She believed he had loved being with her and her family, that they had helped him see the people and the town in a new, better light.

Setting down the phone, she stood and smoothed her palms down the sides of her pants. She had to get on with her life, but first she had to face her family.

The others were in the great room. When Graceann entered, all conversation stopped. They turned and stared at her. She met her sister's gaze. Lorrie blinked and averted her eyes.

"I'll make you something to eat," her mom said, rising from the sofa.

"Sit, Mom. I have something I need to say to all of you." Graceann clasped her hands in front of her, willing calmness into her voice. "I realize now it was foolish and hurtful of me to deceive you. I was thinking only of myself and not what it would do to you."

"Let's put the whole thing behind us," her father said.

Graceann shook her head. "No. I have to say this.

194

I know you love me and I love you. Seeing you this Christmas through Jake's eyes made me realize how very lucky I am to have you." She met her mother's gaze. "Mom, I know you only want what's best for me. And I adore you for it. But I'm able to take care of myself. Please let me live my life on my own terms. Have faith that you raised me right and I know what I'm doing."

Her mother swiped at tears. "I know, dear. It's not always easy to let go, but I'm trying."

"I didn't realize what Mom's matchmaking was doing to you." Lorrie shot a wry smile at her mother. "Sorry, Mom, but you did push some real jerks at Graceann."

Her words provoked soft laughter from the others.

"Are we okay now?" Graceann asked. "I'll live my life my way?"

"We trust you'll do what's right," her dad said. "But don't expect us to stop worrying about you."

Graceann smiled. "I know. And that's okay." She drew a steadying breath. "I have one more thing I need to say."

The others sat quietly, waiting.

"I Googled Jake. He really is an up and comer in Hollywood. He produces and writes indie movies, little-known but well-reviewed. I guess that's why we hadn't heard of him. I may need to go to California. Jake and I have to settle things between us."

"Is that wise? To go after him?" her mother asked. "You should make him chase you."

"This isn't a game, Mom. Not anymore. I'm taking the initiative from now on."

"That's my granddaughter," Grandmom said.

"And my little sister," Lorrie said. "I always knew you were feisty."

Graceann laughed as relief flooded her. Her family understood. They'd support her in whatever she decided.

The doorbell rang, the sound puncturing the quiet and making Graceann jump.

"I'll get it," her dad said.

He hurried out to the entry hall, the rubber soles of his sneakers slapping against the marble floor. The door opened, then her father's voice rang out.

"What are you doing back here?"

Chapter Sixteen

HER HEART THUDDING, Graceann hurried out to the entry hall.

Jake stood on the front step. The stubborn set of his jaw shouted his determination as he faced her father. "Please let me in. I have to see Graceann."

"I don't know if she wants to see you," her father said in a raspy voice.

Graceann understood what her father was doing...he was trying to protect her until she was ready to face Jake. "It's okay, Daddy. I'll talk to him."

Like a balloon pricked with a needle, the fight seemed to leave Jake and he visibly relaxed.

"You're sure?" her father asked.

She nodded.

"Use my office." He turned away without another word, leaving her alone with Jake.

Graceann motioned for Jake to come in. He slipped through the door and shut it behind him. "What are you doing here?" she asked.

"I have to talk to you." He stepped closer. "To explain."

She clenched her hands at her sides, fighting the urge to reach out and touch his stubbled face, to skim her fingers over his full lips. But she wouldn't make this easy for him.

"Please, Graceann, I really need to talk to you."

She turned and strode to the office, not looking to see if he followed, but she heard his soft footsteps close behind. When they got into the other room, she closed the door and went to stand in front of her father's desk. She folded her arms across her chest, as protection from her chaotic emotions.

Jake stood by the door, as if wary of coming too close to her.

"Why did you come back?" she asked.

"I got to my condo and I knew I couldn't walk away from you, not until I had your forgiveness, and maybe a lot more. I threw my bags in my condo, and the driver brought me back here."

He massaged his temple. "Hell, Graceann, I never meant any of this to happen. Please forgive me. I should have told you from the beginning. I was wrong. I should never have agreed to this fiancé

198

charade. Because of me you were humiliated in front of your family."

She gave him a slight smile. "I humiliated myself."

He walked to one of the windows and opened the blinds to stare out, his back to her. Her hungry gaze devoured him. She'd hear him out before she decided if she could forgive him.

Finally, he turned to face her again. "I bungled things badly earlier when I asked you to come to California with me. I was being selfish, wanting to spend more time with you, but not considering you have a life and a career here. I didn't tell you the truth about me, yet I expected you to drop everything and come with me across the country. Some arrogance, huh?"

"Yeah, you were being a little selfish." Her soft voice tempered her words.

His lips tilted in a slight smile. "That's me. Selfish and stubborn. It's not the first time I've done something stupid, and it won't be the last."

She leaned against the edge of the desk. "Is that why you came back—to apologize?"

"That and more. At first, I didn't think the truth about me and what I do would matter. I was playing a role for you and your family." He held her gaze. "My role became real as I found myself falling in love with you. Once I realized how I felt about you, I told myself I wasn't capable of loving anyone and that you deserved better than what I could give you."

Love? Had she heard right?

"I was in denial about my feelings, and I hurt you," he continued, interrupting her thoughts. "The truth hit me on the drive to Bremer. I was more scared of losing you than I was of loving you."

She lowered her gaze as joy wound through her. They still had issues to resolve, but... She picked up a paperweight she'd given her father for Christmas one year. Graceann smiled. She'd been eight and had saved her allowance to buy him something special. A bright yellow flower was trapped inside the thick glass. The petals were opened, as if the bloom was grasping at freedom. Like the flower, Graceann had been trapped by her need to please her parents, her fear of expressing her feelings to them. Unlike the blossom, she was free now. Jake, despite his secrets, had helped free her.

Setting down the paperweight, she met his gaze.

He gave her a tender smile. Her heart stumbled when he smiled like that.

"Will you forgive me, Graceann? Will you give us a chance?"

"I'm trying to understand, Jake. You said you wanted me to care for the real you, and not some hot-shot Hollywood type. I get that now, although I still feel betrayed that you didn't trust me with the truth."

When he started to walk toward her, she held up a hand. "I have more I need to say. I believe you about the movie—that you won't show Spirit Lake in a bad way."

His features softened. "Thanks for that at least."

Drawing a deep breath, she continued. "You were right about me, partially right. I did misjudge you when I asked you to be my pretend fiancé. I assumed you were down on your luck. And truthfully, I was excited at the thought of getting close to The Falcon, the mystery guy of Spirit Lake High. But then I got to know you and everything changed."

"How?" His intense gaze pinned her.

She straightened and clasped her hands in front of her. "I liked what I saw. It didn't matter what type work you did. I realized you're a loving, good-hearted guy."

He gave her a self-deprecating smile. "Are you sure you're talking about me?"

She laughed. "Yes, I'm talking about you, Jake Falco. I Googled you, you know."

"Find anything interesting?"

She exhaled slowly, feeling her tense muscles begin to relax. "I learned you're an up-and-coming indie film producer and screenwriter."

"Who no one's heard of."

"Not yet. I think all that's about to change. There's a lot of buzz about your new zombie film."

"From your lips to God's ears." He moved closer until inches separated them, then he took one of her hands in his. "You haven't said if you'll forgive me."

She wanted to forgive him. She hadn't been honest with her family and they'd forgiven her. She couldn't do less. Her breathing shallow, she nodded. "I do forgive you. We have issues of trust, both of us, but we can work through it."

He squeezed her hand. "I can't let you go, Graceann. I tried to be the hero who would set you free so you could find love with someone worthy of you. I'm no hero. I want you for myself. No matter that you deserve someone better than me, I can't imagine a life without you in it. I'll do my best to make you happy."

"Make me happy?" Anticipation made her heart beat a quick tempo.

"I'm not saying this right. My feelings for you scare the crap out of me. I've never been in love before."

"Maybe you should just say you love me. Is that so hard?"

"I thought I said that."

"You didn't, not in so many words."

Cupping her face between his hands, he said, "I love you, Graceann Palmer. I think I've loved you since that first day in the diner, maybe even before that, but I didn't have the courage to admit it until now."

She smiled. "I love you, too, Jake Falco."

"I know."

With a short laugh, she stepped back and wound her arms around his waist. "Arrogant, as always, I see."

"Not really. I was petrified you wouldn't forgive me and would send me packing." He skimmed a finger over her lips. "I heard you tell Steven I'm twice the man he is. And I knew you wouldn't have given yourself so freely to me if you didn't love me. That's who you are. And that's one of the many things I love about you."

He kissed her softly, as if wanting to savor her. When the kiss ended, he gave her a long, searching look from eyes that sparkled with love. "I never believed in love before you, never thought I was capable of it. You opened my eyes and my heart. I love you more than I thought it was possible to love anyone. Marry me, Graceann. Start a life and a family with me. All those things I told myself I didn't want, but deep down I craved. I want them all now, with you, only you." His voice softened to a husky whisper. "Please say yes."

They still had issues. She barely knew him, yet her heart leapt for joy at his words. She wanted him, needed him, in her life.

"Yes, I'll marry you."

"You will?"

The sound of her laughter floated through the room as joy filled her heart. "I just said I would."

He gathered her to him and crushed her lips against his in a kiss that poured out his love and branded her as his. She clung to him, eager and hungry for the man she would love forever.

When the kiss ended, she pulled away, her breathing ragged, and stroked his face. "Santa brought me the best gift ever. My very own groom for Christmas."

Epilogue

Two years later

Snuggling closer to her husband, Graceann took Jake's hand in hers as they rode in the back of the limo. The darkening city of Los Angeles, decked out for Christmas, blurred past, casting a colorful collage of white, green, and red lights on the tinted windows. Graceann sighed and squeezed Jake's hand.

"Happy?" he asked, smiling down at her.

"Delirious." She returned his smile.

He patted her seven-months pregnant belly. "How's little Jake doing?"

"I think he's calmer than I am about attending his first Hollywood premiere."

"You'll do fine. The paparazzi love you. The camera loves you. I love you." He brushed a whisper soft kiss on her lips. "You weren't nervous last week at the worldwide premiere in Spirit Lake."

"That was more of a hometown event, no red carpet, and there were only a few photographers. And you and your movie were a big hit. I don't believe the town's ever had that kind of excitement." Jake had rented out the largest movie theater in town and invited the townspeople. True to his word, Jake's romantic comedy zombie movie, *Night of the Loving Dead*, showed Spirit Lake and its people in a good light.

"Maybe we'll have the world premiere of my next movie there again."

She shot him a wry smile. "And maybe I won't be big as a house. My first Hollywood premiere and I'm huge." She smoothed a hand over the skirt of her red silk gown.

Jake leaned closer and trailed fingers along her cleavage, exposed by the low-cut neckline. "You get more beautiful every day. Pregnancy agrees with you."

Married one year ago on the afternoon of Christmas Eve in the church at Spirit Lake, Jake never failed to excite her. Even now, pregnant and riding in the back of a limo, she wanted him.

"You look amazing in that dress," he said. "But I can't wait to get you out of it."

"You look amazing in that tux, and I can't wait to get you out of it."

He laughed and tucked her arm through his. "I hope there are many more children in our future. And many more movie premieres." A note of nervousness had crept into his voice.

"There will be, for both. I want lots of children with you. And you'll make more hit movies. You're a talented writer and a savvy producer."

He lifted her hand and kissed it. "You'd compliment me no matter what because you love me."

"I love you so much my heart is ready to burst. But I wasn't merely giving you a compliment. The movie really is great. You're already getting glowing reviews, and not just from your adoring wife."

Blinking back tears of happiness, she looked at her left hand resting on her belly. The emerald stone in her engagement ring twinkled in the soft overhead lighting. She turned her hand, letting the light catch the facets of the large gem. Jake had had a jeweler friend make the emerald and diamond ring, an exact copy of the faux engagement ring she'd made. The jeweler was so impressed with her design, he'd hired her as a designer for his shop on Rodeo Drive. Thanks to Jake's contacts in the movie industry, she had a thriving jewelry business of her own. The female lead in Jake's movie wore jewelry designed by Graceann.

With a contented sigh, Graceann turned her attention back to the cityscape unfolding before her.

Her family rode in the limo behind them. Christmas Eve was in a few days. Kate and Zach were flying in tomorrow to spend the holidays with them. Graceann hoped her two best friends could be civil to each other on the long flight. She loved them dearly but whenever they were in the same room, sparks flew.

She and Jake would celebrate their wedding anniversary and the holidays with her family and her two friends. The house they'd bought in the Hollywood Hills was big enough to accommodate everyone. Graceann's studio was in a small cottage on the sprawling grounds.

Grandmom had left Fluffy home with a friend, thinking it best to protect the little dog from Jake's cats, Sasha and Tasha. The cats were bigger than the dog and wouldn't take kindly to sharing space with him.

Graceann's whole family, including her mother, loved Jake. She glanced at her handsome husband, so striking in his tuxedo. No one loved Jake more than she did.

In the past year they'd given each other the life Graceann had always envisioned and the family life Jake had never dared to dream he could have.

The limo pulled up to the theater. A crowd waited behind the velvet ropes. When the driver opened the car door for them, flashbulbs went off. Jake got out first, then reached for Graceann's hand to help her out. She slipped her arm through his as they walked along the red carpet, smiling for the fans lined up to watch.

As they passed a group of teenage girls, one said, "He's so dreamy."

"He's hot," said another.

Jake leaned down and kissed Graceann lightly on the lips. "And he's so in love with his wife. I love you, my Christmas bride."

"And I love you, my Christmas groom."

Books by Cara Marsi

A Catered Romance
A Cat's Tale & Other Love Stories
A Cinderella Christmas
A Groom for Christmas
Accidental Love
Cursed Mates
Logan's Redemption (Redemption Book 1)
Franco's Fortune (Redemption Book 2)
Love Potion
Loving Or Nothing
Murder, Mi Amore
Storm of Desire
The Ring

Read excerpts at www.CaraMarsi.com
All books available at online booksellers
Loving Or Nothing and Murder, Mi Amore are also
available in print

All About Award-Winning Author Cara Marsi

I'm a former corporate drone and cubicle dweller with a romantic soul. I crave books with happy endings and I love to write about independent, feisty women and the sexy, strong guys who love them. I also love to put my characters in dangerous situations and situations that are merely dangerous to their hearts and watch them fight for the happy endings they deserve.

I credit my love of romance to the old Thirties and Forties romantic comedies I watched on late night TV growing up. I'm published in contemporary romance, romantic suspense, paranormal romance, and I've also published numerous short romance stories in national magazines. My husband and I enjoy traveling and I love to write about the places we've visited. We share our house with a fat black diva of a cat named Killer.

I hope you enjoyed A Groom for Christmas. I really appreciate your purchase. Find out more about me and my other books at my website at CaraMarsi.com.

I'm on Twitter, Goodreads, Facebook, and Pinterest. I'm always interested in meeting new friends.

Made in the USA
Lexington, KY
04 September 2014